UNFORGOTTEN

STORIES of STRONG WOMEN

Betsey Barber Hampton

UNFORGOTTEN, Stories of Strong Women
COPYRIGHT @ 2019 by Betsey Barber Hampton

Cover art: Betsey Hampton

Merlin-Janus Studio, Inc.

Mooresville, NC

Publishing History

First Edition 2019

Print ISBN: 978-0-578-50894-8

Published in the United States of America

UNFORGOTTEN

One of the strongest women I know is my friend,
Maddie Jean Clark.
A special thanks to her
for her assistance with these stories
and her inspiration and support
in countless ways.

ALEXANDRA

Putting "Alex" on my application to Dixon College wasn't untruthful at all. That's what Uncle Sid and his archeological students called me. I had always been one of the boys wearing boy clothes, a boy haircut, and I loved digging in the dirt and bathing in the river.

When I turned sixteen my little hormone factories let me in on a secret, so when I showed up at Dixon for biology 101, I had mastered the art of femininity. I wore a dress, curled my hair and used lipstick.

Professor Thiel stroked his mustache, adjusted his bow tie, fixed his steely blue eyes on me and asked, "Young lady, what are you doing here?"

I licked my bright red lips, which had gone quite dry. "I'm here for your class, sir."

"You have made a mistake. This is an all-male school," he announced in distain.

I could feel my cheeks burn. "Excuse me, sir, I *am* on your list. Here, let me show you." I pointed to the first name on his list, Alex Ames.

***

My parents died in an accident when I was five, and Uncle Sid, Daddy's brother, raised me. He was an archeologist who graduated from Dixon and from UNC. I don't remember much about my parents. My father looked a lot like Uncle Sid. I recall how my mother smelled when she rocked me to sleep as I sucked my thumb, wound my fingers through her long black hair and looked into eyes like pools of black ink.

The only home I can remember is our tent: mine and Uncle Sid's. It went everywhere with us, all over the country, really, wherever he went for a dig. I almost never slept in a bed. I had a bedroll, a backpack for my clothes and few belongings. *Things* didn't matter to me or to my uncle, but the one thing he insisted on was my education, so Dr. Sidney H. Ames didn't accept a dig until he made sure we were near a school and transportation was provided.

We ate meat caught in the wild and cooked over a fire. I learned how to gather mushrooms, berries, greens and roots. Besides their nutritional value, I was interested in their medicinal value.

When Uncle Sid died from pneumonia, I was devastated. An antibiotic would have saved him, but we were too far in the wild and there wasn't time to get him to a doctor. That's when I knew what I would do with my life.

In his will, he left me a lot of money to be used for a college education. He left Dixon College $10,000, provided they enroll me as the first female student.

So, here I was standing in front of grouchy old Lawrence Thiel, who wanted nothing more than to make me go away. There were muffled snickers and sneers from the room filled with smug male students, who looked down their noses at me and laughed at the idea of a female in their midst – all except Joseph Locklear, also an outsider, who smiled and motioned for me to sit beside him.

Joe, a Lumbee Indian who came to Dixon on a football scholarship, was shunned at first. But soon he became a football hero and my only friend.

His girlfriend, Cree, a Cherokee, was forbidden by her clan to associate with a Lumbee, so when she wanted to visit Joe, she stayed with me in my garage apartment.

Cree invited me to spend holidays with her and her grandmother Lura, a medicine woman, who taught me how to heal with herbs.

When Joe and I graduated from Dixon, he got a job coaching at a small school in the North Carolina mountains. I enrolled in UNC School of Medicine, where I would become a surgeon. Again, I was the only female student and not well received by my professors and fellow students. But my grades were good, and I was the niece of Dr. Sidney H. Ames, distinguished alumni and former professor.

In my second week at UNC, I was approached by a graduate archeological student who told me that when he was a freshman he went on a dig with Uncle Sid and remembered his teenage tomboy niece.

Harrison Fuller invited me to come by the history and artifacts museum. "We have most of your uncle's collection and a lot of personal memorabilia that he donated to us."

Memories flooded my mind as I looked at the glass cases of artifacts. I saw fluted arrowheads, probably made by the Iroquois, a pink quartz arrowhead that I found myself, the hammer stone I had rubbed my fingers over wondering who had used it and for what.

Harrison disappeared into a locked room and returned with a box labeled *SIDNEY H. AMES,* which he placed on a worn oak table and pulled out a chair for me. My hands trembled as I opened the box to see what secrets it held.

Inside were newspaper articles, photos of Uncle Sid on various digs, and at the very bottom was a faded blue book – his diary.

Skipping over to his last year at UNC, I read about his favorite classes, professors, assignments and the fun and excitement of going on digs with his classmates:

Monday, March 26: *Professor Charles Mason and a group of us set out on a three week dig to find Indian relics. We set up camp in the early morning and began to uncover a site we believed to have been a tribal home.*

There were pottery shards I suspect were made by Tuscaroras. My friends and I spent hours sifting soil through screens, discovering perfect arrowheads and pieces of tomahawks that I believe were also made by the Tuscaroras , a waring tribe..

Tuesday, March 27: *Late in the afternoon I wandered ahead and became separated from the group. Thinking I knew my way to our camp, I kept walking until my foot slipped on damp leaves and I found myself at the bottom of a ravine, suffering from a sprained ankle and a skinned and bleeding knee.*

By hanging on to vines, I made my way to the top and called out to my classmates, who were already out of hearing distance. Then I sat in stunned silence under a cloudless sky watching wisps of smoke rising in the distance, above the pine trees and scrub. I was facing the night alone and in pain – a night that was quickly getting close to dark.

And then I saw her coming through the trees. She stopped her horse beside me. "You hurt?"

"Yes, and lost."

"You are you in pain?" she asked, and then knelt beside me to check my wounds. "Come, let me help you on my horse. My grandmother will make a poultice of mullin for your ankle."

"But I need to find my camp," I said.

"Tomorrow."

And with that, the woman named Mira, helped me onto her horse and headed toward her village.

Lura, her grandmother, soaked the mullin in hot water and plastered it on my aching ankle. She cleaned my knee and rubbed it with goose grease before handing me a bowl of rabbit stew, corn cake and sassafras tea.

March 28: *Dawn was a blush in the trees when Mira and I headed through the forest the next morning to find my camp.*

I rode behind her holding her waist and smelling the sweetness of her hair as it blew across my face. I was almost sorry when I reached my friends and had to say goodbye. Sliding off the horse and being careful not to put weight on my ankle, I said, "I'll see you again. I must thank you and your grandmother properly."

April 5: *Took candy and cookies to Mira and her grandmother. Mira seemed happy to see me.*

May 1: *Have made several trips to see Mira. Haven't been able to get her off my mind. Took her home to meet Mama and Daniel.*

May 26: *Graduated with honors. Now a PhD. Have a job teaching at UNC.*

November 1: *Thinking about my future: marrying, settling down, starting a family. But my job comes first, and my schedule is to take my students on a dig in late November, return by Christmas, time to think about asking Mira to marry me.*

December 23: *Excited to be home, to see Mama. Have decided to ask Mira to be by wife. Parked in front of the house. The usual wreath wasn't on the door. Mama always had a Christmas tree with loads of colored lights and ornaments that my brother Daniel and I had collected through the years, but there was no tree. There were no sweet aromas of fruit cakes and Christmas cookies coming from the kitchen. Mama looked sad. Surely my brother would have gotten in touch if she were ill.*

I asked where Daniel was.

"They moved out."

"They?"

"He and Mira."

So, there it was.

December 24: *Blind with anger, I went back to UNC and immersed myself in work.*

May 14: *Mama called to say that Daniel and Mira's baby had been born - a girl named Alexandra.*

October 30: *On orders from Mama, I went home for the christening. She told me in no uncertain terms that it was time I got over my anger and faced reality. This child was not responsible for what her parents did. I was her uncle and it was time I started acting like it.*

The first time I laid eyes on little Alex, I was smitten. She looked like the Ames side of the family – fair skin and blue eyes. I held out my arms to her and she thrust herself toward me as though she had been waiting for me.

December 25: *My first Christmas with my niece. I gave her her first doll. For that alone, she and I formed a lasting bond.*

I was halfway through a box of Kleenex when I read about the doll. I had slept with that doll until I was six or seven years old. I named her Betty. She had curly blond hair and eyes that opened and shut under her long brown lashes. I don't know what happened to her, but I would like very much to hold her again.

I skipped to where Uncle Sid wrote about my parent's death and how he came for me, wondering how he would manage a small child in his line of work. I had already cried until there were no tears left in me. I placed the faded book back in the box and made my way home.

I had no idea that my mother was Cherokee, or that Uncle Sid had been in love with her. I learned that my grandmother Elvira and Cree's grandmother Lura were sisters. Elvira married a Scottish immigrant, Ian Kerr, and Lura married Lone Wolf. My mother Mira Kerr and Cree's mother Creola were first cousins, making Cree and me second cousins.

Harrison, the young man who had shown me Uncle Sid's diary, became a good friend. We saw a lot of each other until graduation. I took a job in a hospital in Asheville, while Harrison continued teaching at UNC.

Cree was also working in Asheville, and I moved into her apartment. She and Joe were to be married on a warm spring afternoon by the Justice of the Peace. I had emergency room duty and was to join them to be a witness after I got off work at 3:00.

I had set a broken leg, stitched the hand of a construction worker, made afternoon rounds and had just sat down at my desk to catch my breath when I was summoned to the ER again.

My new patient was covered with blood. One eye had a gash above it. He had a swollen jaw, both legs were broken and there were bruises around his back and abdomen. I ordered x-rays and had him prepped for surgery. I left to go scrub.

When I entered the surgery, the patient had already been anesthetized and placed on a breathing tube. My bruised and battered patient was Joe Locklear.

Joe was going to be fine. One of his legs would be slightly shorter than the other, but he was a lucky man to have survived such a horrible ordeal.

We suspected someone from the Cherokee nation had perpetrated the attack in objection to their marriage – maybe even Cree's family members.

She and Joe asked the hospital chaplain to marry them in his room. When he was discharged, Cree and I took him home to begin his long recovery.

In the meantime, I got a call from Dr. Harrison Fuller. He was coming to Asheville to attend an archeological meeting and invited me to have dinner with him at a local restaurant. I had forgotten how incredibly handsome he was. His auburn hair was worn in a ponytail. He was tanned from the North Carolina sun, taller than I remembered, and toned like an athlete.

We spent a lot of time catching up before he got around to telling me the reason for our meeting.

"Alex, don't say anything before you take some time to consider my offer. I take students out into the wild for weeks, where no medical care is available, and I fear I'm placing them in danger. I would like for you to join me. You would be working for UNC and on their payroll. The salary would be much less than you could make on your chosen career path. The University will provide as much equipment as we can manage to transport. It's a lot to ask Alex, but you, of all people, know the obstacles involved. You are the perfect person for this challenge."

Uncle Sid had prepared me for this. I could do it. So I sent a message to Harrison the following week saying it would be an honor to accept his offer.

I left my few belongings with Joe and Cree and joined Harrison in the wilderness. It felt like I had come home.

The arrangement worked beautifully: my career and my eventual marriage to Harry. When we retired, we bought a mountain overlooking Ashville and built a modest home. Our camping equipment was always handy for when we got the urge to sleep under the stars. Unfortunately, Harry developed arthritis and had to give up camping.

I made a vegetable garden and an herb garden. Our woods were filled with wild plants that I gathered and used for healing, including mullin for Harry's aching joints.

I do miss being in the wild and cooking on an open fire, but I have learned my way around an electric stove.

We have two sons: Harrison, Jr and Sidney Ames Fuller. Harrison is a professor at Black Mountain College and the father of two boys. Sidney has a Christmas tree farm on our mountain. He and his wife have three little girls, all have been added to my list of people to spoil. I can see my Cherokee ancestry when I look at their black hair and eyes like pools of black ink.

I still don't care about material things. My joy comes from listening to the whippoorwills in the woods behind our house, watching the big orange ball of sun slowly drop behind our mountain and waiting for Harry to bring the glass of wine that we share every evening. I know he will pull me close, kiss my forehead and whisper, "I love you, Alexandra."

BESSIE

Miss Bessie yelled out the back door, "Jeanie, Jeanie, I need you! Come up here."

I put on a clean dress and started up the hill to Gifford's. They lived in a little white house on South Street, with a screened porch on the front and one on the back. Mr. Grant Gifford was sittin' on the back steps. His bald head glistened in the afternoon sun like a fishin' float. His cat Blue was by his side.

He was a short, stooped little man who always wore tan shirts and khaki trousers held up by red suspenders. He had a hacking cough, probably from all the Chesterfields he smoked. Mr. Grant hardly ever opened his mouth, but he looked up with his little rabbit eyes, and in his soft, squeaky voice said, "How you, Jeanie?"

I opened the door to the back porch and noticed Mr. Grant's cot hadn't been changed since the last time I did it, so I figured I best start a load of laundry in the Maytag.

When I entered the kitchen, I almost tripped on the cartons of empty Coke bottles, old boxes and newspapers Miss Bessie had stacked inside the door. She claimed this trash *would come in handy someday*.

Blue took this opportunity to run in between my legs, where he knew good and well he wadn't spose to be, but he loved to get under Miss Bessie's skin. That cat knew what was comin' next:

"Git your mangy butt out of my house before I kill you!" Miss Bessie hollered from the sittin' room.

When I looked around, I thought, *Oh, Lord. Ain't no wonder she called me!* The sink was full of dirty dishes, an empty Jiffy peanut butter jar and some plastic containers that Miss Bessie was *savin' for a rainy day.* From the mess, I guessed Miss Bessie was in her rockin' chair with a Coke in one hand and peanut butter crackers in the other, watchin' *I Love Lucy* on TV.

Sure 'nuff, she belched loud enough for me to hear it clean back in the kitchen before she come struttin' in to boss me 'round. She moved just like a turkey, always wore flowery dresses under an apron. She wore her hair twisted into a scrawny little knot on top of her head. Her readin' glasses hung on a chain 'round her long skinny turkey neck.

Good Lord Almighty, she didn't need to tell me what to do. I'd already figured that out on my own. I had run hot water in the blue enamel dish pan and squirted in some Palmolive Liquid.

While I worked, Mr. Grant finished his cigarette and went down to his shop in the basement. I could hear his saw runnin'. He was makin' one of his pine caskets. It smelled like pine, anyway.

The word around Dixon was that Mr. Gifford moved here from Pennsylvania. Before that, they say his folks come over from Germany. His daddy and even his granddaddy before him were woodworkers who made furniture and caskets.

Folks around town loved to own a piece of Mr. Grant's furniture—but caskets, not so much. Yet the truth was, some folks couldn't afford the fancy ones the funeral parlor displayed in their showroom. Mr.

Grant, kind hearted as he was, made plain wooden caskets for people who didn't have much money, and the Cashions always kept one or two on hand at their funeral parlor. So did the Calvins in Moorestown.

Some strange people lived in Dixon, and the Giffords were at the top of that list. Mister and Missus didn't have nothin' to do with each other. Now that sounds strange, but so help me, it's God's own truth. Well I guess they got along once upon a time, 'cause they had a daughter, Mary Alice, who lived up in the mountains near Morganton.

Poor Mr. Grant tried so hard to please his wife, but there just wadn't nothin' he did that suited the woman. Every year when he planted his garden he planted zinnias for her. When lightning struck the old walnut tree in the backyard, he had the wood cut and made a bedside table for her to keep her pill bottles on. She claimed it wadn't level. She said the bottles rolled off and told him to get the damned thing out of her house.

"That fool can't do nothin' right," Miss Bessie complained. "He hadn't got no more sense than a squirrel waiting for a car to come before it runs into the street."

But their daughter, Mary Alice, sure did love her Daddy. On his birthday, she gave him a kitten. He had a red collar with a little bell. He was gray, but in the sunlight he looked blue, so Mr. Grant named him Blue.

Miss Bessie had the reputation for being the meanest woman in town, and she come by that honest enough. She didn't have nothing to do with nobody, not even her neighbors Miss Cantwell and Miss Cashion, who tried to be nice to her.

Poor Mr. Grant mostly lived on the back porch because Miss Bessie didn't want him in the house, and that suited him just fine. He covered the screen with heavy duty plastic, slept on a cot and kept warm with a little kerosene heater. He watched *Gunsmoke, Gilligan's Island* and *Little House on the Prairie* on a tiny Motorola TV.

When she felt like it, Miss Bessie turkey strutted, her feet shuffling in old black bedroom slippers, out to the porch. She brought old leftover food and put it in on a tray in front of Mr. Grant's TV. Now, I know for a fact that Miss Cantwell and Miss Cashion felt sorry for the poor man and brought him his favorite foods, which Miss Bessie refused to give him.

Miss Janie Cashion was a widow and made a livin' sewin' for the public. Mr. Grant paid Miss Janie to make the quilted satin linings for his caskets. Her house was next door to the Gibson's, with a picket fence between them. Nosy Miss Bessie watched out her bedroom window when Miss Cashion met Mr. Grant at the fence to bring him a finished lining.

The only time Mr. Grant went inside was when he needed to use Miss Bessie's bathroom. She never set foot in his workshop, said it was spooky down there. She swore he buried bodies under the front porch.

One day I had just finished drying the dishes when Miss Bessie come in the kitchen and told me to start on the ironing. She had sprinkled some clothes, rolled them in a towel and put them in the ice box.

"Jeanie," she said, "you hear that pounding? That's them dead people up under the porch."

I took a deep breath. "No ma'am, that's only Mr. Grant hammering."

"Well, just listen. Can't you hear them moanin' and groanin'?"

"No, Miss Bessie. That's only Mr. Grant's sander."

The woman was crazy and she scared me half to death, but Mary Alice was payin' me to keep an eye on them. She was especially concerned about her daddy.

I finished the ironing and went to hang Miss Bessie's dresses in her closet. Well, that wadn't no easy thing. All the clothes she'd ordered from Sears Roebuck over the years were hangin' in there. What I couldn't put on a hanger, I stacked on the chest of drawers and the chairs. I saw a pile of magazines beside her bed that was older than me.

One warm day the end of August, Miss Bessie told me to come help her make scuppernong jelly. Mr. Grant had a bushel basketful of berries sittin on the back steps when I arrived. He always kept scuppernong vines and a wonderful garden. The pantry shelves were already lined with green beans, tomatoes and chow chow that I helped Miss Bessie can.

She was watchin' *Queen for a Day* when I walked in.

"I just ain't myself today Jeannie," she said. "Them people from under the porch kept me awake all night. They was out in the front yard dressed in long white robes. They was carryin' lanterns and dancin' around singing: *Here we go round Bessie's bush, Bessie's bush, Bessie's bush... Here we go round Bessie's bush so early in the morning – boo Bessie!"*

I ignored her, and soon we had the scuppernongs a boilin' and I was scaldin' the jars. I had the sieve lined with muslin ready to strain out the hulls and seeds when I heard Mr. Grant calling, "Here kitty, kitty! Blue, where are you Blue?"

We filled the jars and poured melted paraffin on top to seal in the jelly. Miss Bessie lined 'em up in the kitchen window to cool. The afternoon sun was shinin' though the jars, making little pink shapes all over the kitchen sink when I heard somebody talkin' to Mr. Grant.

"My goodness, Grant, there was a dead cat in that casket you brought up here this morning." The voice belonged to Mr. Reid Cashion, from over at the funeral parlor. "I hate to say it, but it looked like your cat, Grant. Had a little red collar with a bell on it."

Mr. Grant blinked back tears. "All right, I'll be up there directly and see to it, Reid.

The next mornin' a police woke me up knockin' on my door. He said Mary Alice wanted me to go stay with her mama till she come down from Morganton. Actually, I'd rather been dead in a ditch than go back up to the Gifford's, but I knew Mary Alice was countin' on me.

I found Miss Bessie sittin' in front of her TV watchin' *Art Linkletter*, her face was the color of goose turds.

"Oh, my Lord in heaven, am I glad to see you, Jeannie! I'm so mad, I don't know what to do. Them dead people from under the porch was out there singin' all night. I didn't sleep a wink."

"What was they singin', Miss Bessie?"

"They wore them long white robes and carried their damned lanterns. They was dancin' round and round singin', *Sing me a song of a cat that is gone. Say, could that cat be Blue? Poor little kitty ate poison one day, fed to him by guess who? Boo, Bessie, boo!*

"After that," Miss Bessie continued, "I called the police and they come early this mornin'. They had Dr. Forest with them. Damned fools, all of them. Dr. Forest gave me some kind of shot and told me to keep calm till Mary Alice come down from Morganton. Lord, ain't nobody gets on my nerves more than Mary Alice."

It wadn't no more than an hour before Mary Alice's car pulled up outside, along with Dr. Forest and a police, who put Miss Bessie in the back of his car.   Mary Alice ran into Miss Bessie's bedroom, grabbed a suitcase and started throwing stuff in it.

"Jeanie," she said, "I'm taking Mama to Morganton and she won't be coming back. Git all this clutter out of the house and put mama's clothes in some boxes. Help Daddy move his stuff inside and make up the bed, so he can sleep in it tonight and every night from now on. Rest assured, there will be no more ghosts in long white robes traipsing around the front yard."

"Jeanie, you take good care of my daddy," Mary Alice said as she was runnin' out the door to follow the police car to Morganton. "Daddy," she yelled, "Blue has a little sister named Sweetie Pie. She needs a good home and somebody to love her. I'll bring her with me when I come back. Bye, Daddy, love you."

Well, it took me three whole days to get rid of all that junk in the house. I helped Mr. Grant load it in the back of his '48 green Ford pickup truck to haul to the dump. The house looked real nice when I got it all cleaned up.

Mary Alice was so happy when she come down and brought Sweetie Pie. I still go over once a week to clean and do Mr. Grant's laundry, and I cook some too.

Now there's a pretty embroidered tablecloth and most always leftovers in the ice box. Now don't get me wrong. I ain't the type to be nosy and go 'round spreadin' tales on people, and I'm pretty sure Miss Cashion is just being a good neighbor, 'cause that's what folks in Dixon do. But judgin' from the smile on Mr. Grant's face these days— and I ain't the only one seen it—he's got a new woman in his life.

And I 'spect everybody's thinkin' the same as me – *It's about damn time!*

BONNIE

Thursday was my day to clean for Miss Bonnie White. She was still in bed when I got there at 9:00. She got home late last night because she was starring in a play downtown. Mr. White was still in bed too, but not the same bed, and not even the same bedroom.

When I looked in his neat little bedroom to see if I could change his sheets, he scared me half to death, lying there like a dead man with the covers pulled over his head. He always lined his shirts up on one side of the closet, his pants on the other and his shoes in a neat row on the floor.

Miss Bonnie's bedroom? Oh, my lord, that was another matter. You couldn't see the bed under the piles of clothes and costumes. Just walking in there made me crazy and she didn't want me touchin' nothin'. The floor was covered with hats, wigs, capes, parasols, shoes, stockings and underwear. The dressing table was covered with jars of creams, jewelry and an ashtray full of cigarette butts covered with bright red lipstick.

Miss Bonnie always did her grocery shopping on Saturday. She never emptied the bags or put the food away. Wadn't no way she needed to bother, 'cause she didn't do the cooking. So I went through the bags and threw away what was spoiled, carried it outside to the garbage can and put up the rest.

The only thing Miss Bonnie cared much about besides the theater and her acting was her cat, Tallulah, who hadn't been fed in God knows when. I opened a can of cat food and emptied it into her bowl and then emptied the litter box.

By then Mr. White was up. I heard him flush his toilet. Pretty soon he worked his way down the stairs stepping over the stage costumes and wigs Miss Bonnie had dropped around when she got home last night. He was wearing an emerald green satin shirt, a gold chain around his neck, and he was stuffed into tight black pants. He was out the door and into his car before you could bat an eye, probably on his way to see Mr. Conroy.

Next Miss Bonnie got up. I could hear her practicing her lines. I was in the front hall when she started downstairs, a cigarette dangling out one side of her mouth. Her hair? Well, the way it looked when she came out of the shower was the way it stayed. Her red shawl was draped around her shoulders. Her shoes with little spike heels were too big for her feet and made a flip floppin' sound as she started down the stairs.

Miss Bonnie flung her shawl over her left shoulder, drew on her cigarette, blew a puff of smoke out over the stairwell and in her husky voice said, "All right, I'm ready for my close-up. Stop telling me I'm *yesterday's* glamour queen, Cecil. I'm big as ever—it's the pictures that got smaller."

She went to the kitchen, dug into a couple of grocery bags and said, "Jeannie, where's that grapefruit I bought?"

"It's in the garbage, Miss Bonnie."

"Oh, shit! Then open a can of Beanie Weenies for me and get me that black wig off the stairs."

I got the wrong wig and had to go back. "I'm going to be late!" she screaked and marched across my just mopped floor in her spikey little heels. She threw her red shawl over her shoulder and flew out the door like a well-oiled grease fire.

I mopped the floor again and then went upstairs to change the sheets. I was puttin' them in the washin' machine when Mr. White and Mr. Conroy came in. Mr. White's first name was Ashe. But Miss Bonnie said it nasty, without the "he" on the end.

Mr. Ashe had his hand on Mr. Conroy's butt, leadin' him into the sittin' room where they were gonna practice what they would play and sing Easter Sunday over at the Methodist church.

Mr. Ashe was the choir director and played the organ. Mr. Conroy sang in the choir. He had the sweetest voice I ever heard. Mr. Ashe played the introduction to Halleluiah, then Mr. Conroy joined in with Halleluiah, Halleluiah, Halleluiah, Halleluiaaaah.

Suddenly, I got this picture in my head of how it will be on Sunday – a choir dressed in white robes, sun shinin' through stained-glass windows sendin' out the most beautiful colors. I could almost smell the Easter lilies placed around the organ. You can hear a pin drop as Mr. Ashe arranges the sheet music in front of him. His long fingers strike the keys. Mr. Conroy rises, steps out front, brushes back his blond hair, waits for Mr. Ashe's' nod, and then starts singin' Halleluiah.

At the same time, I pictured Miss Bonnie at home layin' up in bed, probably under a pile of costumes and probably getting' makeup all over my clean sheets.

The next Thursday at Miss Bonnie's, I emptied the grocery bags, went to the sittin' room, opened the drapes and saw vases of flowers on the table. I also saw an ashtray full of cigarette butts and Miss Bonnie's shoes with the spikey little heels right where she had kicked them off.

I picked up the newspapers that were spread all over the floor and found an article Miss Bonnie had cut out to paste in her scrapbook: *Local Actress Nails Part in Sunset Boulevard.*

A few minutes later, Miss Bonnie opened her bedroom door and yelled, "Millie, make me a pot of coffee."

I had the kitchen pretty well straightened up when she came downstairs, puffing on a cigarette. She poured herself a cup of coffee and said, "Ass has moved out. He and Conroy bought a house together." She started coughing and crying uncontrollably.

"I'm so sorry. Miss Bonnie. You're really gonna miss him."

"Miss Ass? Like hell. That son-of-a-bitch ran over Tallulah!" she said between coughing spasms. "He killed her backing his U-Haul out the driveway."

Turned out, *Sunset Boulevard* would be Miss Bonnie's last real performance. Over the years I worked for her, her voice got so raspy she was unable to act. Instead, she started teaching drama and founded a children's theatre she named *Fiddlesticks Players.*

She had me come two days a week instead of one. Her children's group was a huge success, but it took a toll on her. The group began to tour and play in schools around the area. Miss Bonnie worked longer hours, rested less, smoked more and coughed all the time. Some days she could hardly talk.

On the days I went to work for her, I was afraid of what I might find. She would drag herself out of bed, light up a cigarette, and try to find enough energy to make her way downstairs. She almost never showered anymore, and I didn't have the nerve to tell her that she smelled.

She would drink three or four cups of coffee, eat a piece of toast and leave the house if she was able. Finally, her tired body had had enough. One morning she just sat there and cried.

"I'm sick, Millie." Her deep voice was so raspy I could barely hear.

Soon I was going to Miss Bonnie's three days each week. I got her groceries myself and saw that they were put up right. I cleaned and took care of her and cooked enough to last until I returned.

One night she called me and said in a voice so low I could barely hear, "I can't breathe. I need you Millie!"

When I arrived, I knew I had to call an ambulance. I followed her to the hospital and stayed with her until she died.

Her funeral was held at the Methodist church. Ashe wanted me to be there. I sat on the back row and watched as people filed into the church and filled every pew. There were flowers lining both sides of the vestibule and spread all around the pulpit.

It was a beautiful sunny day, and the sun flowed through the stained-glass windows, across baskets of flowers and onto the pulpit as the minister opened his Bible and read, "The Lord is my shepherd, I shall not want."

Ashe nodded to Conroy, who stepped out in front of the choir and sang *In the Garden.*

The children's choir, dressed in crisp white robes, rose and sang: *All things bright and beautiful, all creatures great and small, the Lord God made them all. Each little flower that opens, each little bird that sings, He made their glowing colors, He made their tiny wings.*

The minister talked about Miss Bonnie—what a shining star she was, a great talent whose fame would never fade. I pictured her standing on the stairs leading to the pearly gates, her red cape around her shoulders, her hair a mess, like she just got out of the shower. With a cigarette hanging out one side of her mouth, she looks down and says, "What did I tell you, Cecil? *Yesterday's* glamour queen? Hell, it's the picture that's got smaller. I'm as big as ever!"

CAROL

CAROL'S COLLECTIBLES was painted in large gold letters across the window of the antique shop located next door to Johnny Brown's department store on Dixon's main street.

The worn, ratty looking teddy bear in the little red rocking chair in the window was irresistible to anyone walking by. A bell on the door rang at the sound of a new customer, and an overpowering wave of incense greeted Millie when she entered. It smelled like a burnt peach cobbler.

The woman behind the counter brushed her bleached blond bangs out of her eyes, looked up from the cloth flowers she was making, smiled and said, "I'm Carol. Let me know if I can help you find anything."

Turning down the classical music on the radio beside her, she came around the counter. She was a tall slender woman wearing a red satin blouse tucked into a short sapphire blue skirt with a wide rhinestone belt around her waist. A rainbow of colors flashed across her rhinestone earrings.

As Millie wandered around the antiques, she spied a sideboard with a mirror on it like one her grandmother used to have. A vase of pink fabric roses stood in front of the mirror, along with a deviled egg dish, a wash bowl and pitcher painted with little purple violets—all like Granny's.

Millie was going through a basket of old jewelry when Carol walked over and asked if she knew of anyone she could hire to clean her house.

"Well, yes ma'am, I can do it," answered Millie

Millie arrived at Carol's the next morning at 8 am and let out a scream when a dog the size of a horse jumped on her.

"Oh, he won't hurt you," Carol said. "Dolly, be a sweet doggie and go lie down. Dolly meandered over to a sofa already covered with dog hair and jumped on.

Huge fabric roses, bows and ribbons hung from the chandelier. They were draped along the curtain rods and across the chairs. They came in all colors and sizes.

The dining room table held bottles of glue, paint and bolts of white fabric from which Carol cut rose petals and leaves. Then she painted them, threaded a wire through them and wound the stems with green floral tape.

China, crystal, lamps and nick knacks were everywhere. Millie figured she bought these things at yard and estate sales to sell in CAROL'S COLLECTIBLES.

Carol left the house to open her shop for the day, leaving Millie to clean around the clutter and to cope with the monstrous dog.

Carol's antique bed was so big Millie could barely walk around it to change the sheets. It had four tall posts covered with a gold fringed canopy reeking with dust. Carol bragged about it having belonged to Queen Elizabeth the First. *Well, not everyone can say they've breathed royal dust,* mused Millie under her breath.

Suddenly she heard the back door open and a man called her name. He was a fat little man, neatly dressed in a dark blue pin stripped suit. It looked like he parted his hair with a water pick and slicked it down with axel grease.

"You are Millie, I believe. I am Cornell, Carol's son."

Suddenly he turned red as a beet and started gasping for breath. When he could speak again, he said, "Sorry, I'm allergic to dust and dog hair."

Cornell told her he was a lawyer who lived in Charlotte. Then he pulled an inhaler from his pocket, stuck it in his mouth and took some deep breaths. His eyes were red and squinty, his nose running. He stuck his chubby little fingers down into the same pocket and pulled out a handkerchief, just before a sneezing fit overtook him. Cornell snorted into the handkerchief and blew his nose.

"Millie," he gasped, "Mama is being evicted. Her landlord has given her thirty days to move. Now, she is just oblivious to the seriousness of this situation." Cornell had another coughing spell, cleared his throat and in a hoarse, squeaky little voice said, "It's up to me to see to this, and hell, I ain't got no damn business even being near this Godforsaken place. Now, I know what you're thinking. Why don't we just move all this junk to her shop? Well, Mama's being evicted from the shop, too."

Cornell sniffed hard, tried to swallow, took a deep ragged breath, coughed and said, "Now, I'm going to need *your* help."

Color crept up his neck like a climbing rose. Before she could respond, he made a gagging noise, got up on his short little legs and ran out the door.

"Cornell could irritate Jesus Christ himself!" Carol screamed when she came home that afternoon. "He told my landlord I was closing CAROL'S COLLECTIBLES. He has arranged for that bitch Trudy Morton to auction all my stuff. If he weren't my son, I swear to God I'd kick his ass to Kingdom Come!"

Sure enough, a *Treasurers by Trudy Truck* arrived bright and early the next morning. They began packing in a storage room in the back of the house, where Trudy discovered a small wooden box covered with decals of primroses and baby's breath. It was locked.

"Carol, where's the key to this little box?" she asked.

"I don't have a key. Never did. Just paid five dollars for it at a yard sale. Can't be worth much—full of junk, I suspect."

Trudy pulled a screwdriver from her toolbox and started unscrewing the hinges. Carol watched intently as the last hinge was removed and the top lifted off to reveal old yellowed letters. They were addressed to Miss Elizabeth Seymore, 525 Confederate Ave., Salisbury, NC. They were from Sgt. Randolph Steele, who was serving in the army in Vietnam.

Trudy removed the letters and underneath found a red velvet box containing an engagement ring.

"My God!" exclaimed Carol. "I'll bet someone has been looking for that ring for years."

While the women continued to pack, contemptuous, controlling Cornell, without his mother's knowledge, purchased a condo with his mother's money and arranged for a mover to move Carol there. The condo was in a senior village where only those 55 and older could live. The only amenities it offered were a clubhouse and a pool.

Carol was sad, unhappy, depressed and furious at what her bossy, aggressive son had done. She would not allow him to control her another day. So, she made a plan: she got herself a lawyer, retracted Cornell's power of attorney, removed him from her will, engaged a realtor to list the condo and called the local antique mall to rent a space and get back in business.

Then she dyed her graying hair, swept it on top of her head and held it in place with a rhinestone encrusted comb. She bought the hottest pink lipstick she could find and a pair of gold sandals. She even treated herself to a pedicure.

Next she poured herself a glass of Merlo, propped her feet up and opened the little box of letters. They all started with *Dearest Elizabeth*. Randolph Steele went on to say that he couldn't wait until he was discharged, and then he would come home in June to marry her. His final letter was dated April 25, 1958. The next letter came from Randolph's mother, informing Elizabeth that her fiancé had stepped on a landmine and had been severely wounded.

Randolph had been medevacked to a surgical center on the base and then to the 106th General Hospital in Yokohama, Japan. After that, they sent him to Valley Forge General Hospital in Pennsylvania. When he was well enough to make the trip, he was flown to the VA hospital in Salisbury, where he was fitted with prosthetic legs and rehabilitated. "Elizabeth, you will be able to visit him there and plan your wedding," Randolph's mother finished.

And then Carol opened the little red velvet box and stared at the diamond ring. She guessed there had been no wedding. Where was Randolph? She intended to find out. And before she got involved in another move, she would find him and return the ring.

It had been fifty years since Vietnam. He was likely dead, but she had to know. She called the VA Hospital in Salisbury and learned that he was very much alive. He had established a group home for the handicapped at 400 Brenner Ave. in Salisbury. Medicare paid for their care and for Randolph to hire a nurse, housekeeper and cook.

Carol expected to find a bitter, broken old man, but instead she found him bent over a raised flower bed pruning roses. "Are you Randolph Steele?" she asked?"

A warm smile found its way across his handsome face. He brushed a lock of snow-white hair out of his blue eyes. "Yes, I am," he said.

She handed him the red velvet box. "I think this belongs to you…" She expected him to become teary and sentimental, but instead he slowly opened the little box and exclaimed "Oh, good Lord. I never expected to see this again. Where in the world did you get it?" He laughed.

"I got it at a yard sale."

"Oh, dear me. Well, I'm not surprised. Elizabeth dropped me as soon she learned of my injury. Her parents didn't approve of me anyway. I came from the wrong side of town for the Seymores. Elizabeth ended up marrying a senator and lives in Washington now. Some things happen for the best, you know."

Randolph grabbed a cane and stood upright on his prosthetic legs. "Let's go inside where it's cool and have a glass of iced tea."

A woman in a wheelchair was getting something from the refrigerator when they went in. "This is Gabrielle," Randolph said. "She was injured in a wreck when she was twelve years old. She is one of the brave people who live here. Bravery is contagious, you know."

Randolph poured Carol a glass of tea and motioned for her to sit at a long table where all the residents gathered for meals. Suddenly a nurse appeared to say, "Mr. Steele, I'm leaving to take William to his doctor's appointment."

Carol could hear music coming from the front of the house. It was the Rolling Stone's singing: *You can't always get what you want, you can't always get what you want, you can't always get what you want, but if you try, sometimes you find what you need.*

"Now, Carol," Randolph said, "tell me about you. And by the way, most people call me Randy."

She had been so angry about losing all her things, her house, her antique shop, everything she had loved. Yet here she was sitting across from a man who had no legs listening to The Rolling Stones singing *you can't always get what you want.*

"I guess you might say I have reached a turning point in my life," she said. "I have to find out what I need, but I have no idea what that is."

"Oh, my Lord!" He laughed. "You too?" I just had my seventieth birthday, so I'm trying to find out what a seventy-year-old man needs." He laughed again. "And damned if I know what that is. I do know I'm going to sell this place and retire, and I do know how much I want to continue my hobby of growing roses, but the rest is a mystery to me now."

A woman came through the back door and said, "Good afternoon, Mr. Steele."

"Good afternoon, Viola," he said, then he turned to Carol and whispered, "She's come to cook dinner. I'd ask you to stay, but I know she's making pinto beans and cornbread. Her cornbread's not so bad, but the beans taste like river rocks."

***

Millie had made fried chicken, potato salad, ham biscuits and a big birthday cake for the seventy-first birthday party in the club house behind Carol's condo. There with vases of roses on each guest table - roses that Randy grew in their yard. Carol no longer made artificial roses, now that she had a yard full. Instead, she made potpourri mixing rose petals with lavender and baby's breath.

Cornell did not attend. He couldn't. He was even more allergic to roses than to dust and dog hair. Besides, he couldn't stand Randy Steele. Randy's army training inclined him not to tolerate the likes of Cornell, and he unapologetically defended his bride.

Randy slipped a piece of chicken under the table to Dolly the dog, his new best friend, before he reached for Carol's hand and felt the wedding band and diamond ring on her finger. *If you try, sometimes you find what you need.*

DIANA

His southern drawl made Diana giggle. Pvt. Robbie Davis was from North Carolina, now stationed at Ft. Campbell, Kentucky, on leave before being shipped overseas. Diana, a Red Cross volunteer, was there to entertain the troops.

The tall handsome soldier had dark olive skin, black hair and brown eyes that twinkled when he smiled. Their eyes met as soon as he entered the canteen and he asked her to dance. And what a dancer he was! He was simply amazing! They danced to the lyrics *"I'm comin' home, I've done my time… Now I've got to know what is and isn't mine… If you received my letter tellin' you I'd soon be free… Then you'll know just what to do, if you still want me… If you still want me, tie a yellow ribbon round the ole oak tree.*

The other girls wanted to dance with him, too, but Robbie wouldn't let go of Diana until she promised to go with him to a movie the following night.

It was freezing cold when she arrived at the Town Cinema. He wrapped her in a tight embrace to keep her warm. They watched *On Golden Pond* and he held her hand the whole time.

Afterwards they had a cup of hot chocolate at the corner drugstore before he walked her home and asked her to meet him for dinner the next night.

Before his two-week leave was up, Diana Smith was madly in love with Pvt. Robbie Davis. She couldn't imagine life without him. They spent his last night together at the Empire Hotel.

The next day at the train station, he kissed her, dried her tears, promised to write and to come back to her as soon as he could. When a letter finally arrived, it came from Vietnam. There were three in all, and then no more.

Robbie had been gone two months when Diana knew she was pregnant. Her morning sickness and the panic of not knowing which way to turn was devastating.

At first, she was mad. How could he do this to her? This baby was his! He said he loved her, but he got her pregnant and left her wondering what happened to him.

Maybe he had been injured, maybe he was in an army hospital, maybe he was dead?

She told Jane, her cousin and only confident, who suggested she forget Robbie Davis and go on a blind date with her, her fiancé and his friend Fred Lewis. Fred, a farmer, was a complete bore. He was several years older than Diana and as anxious to find a wife as she was to find a father for her baby. Diana saw him as her only way out of a terrible situation and never told him she was pregnant. They went to a Justice of the Peace at the local court house and said their vows.

Fred knew everything there was to know about birthing farm animals, but nothing at all about babies. When the baby girl was born after seven months with olive skin, coal black hair and dark brown eyes, he never questioned her parentage.

Diana cried for days when she held little Cassie and remembered how much she had once loved Robbie. Now she was stuck with a husband she could barely tolerate and raising Robbie's baby with him.

When Fred came in at night after milking, his overalls were covered with dirt and his shoes with manure. He was gruff and overbearing. All he cared about was what she had cooked for dinner so he could eat and fall asleep in front of the TV.

After her love affair with Robbie, being married to this lump of a man was depressing. She remembered how happy she had been at the Red Cross, so she began volunteering at a medical assistant program for low income mothers.

Sometime later, Fred came down with flu and became very sick. His doctor told him to stay in and take care of himself, but nobody could tell Fred Lewis what to do. He figured he knew more than just about anybody concerning just about everything.

He was home in bed when Diana went to Cassie's graduation without him. She found herself wondering what Robbie would have thought of his daughter if he were still alive. Cassie was so much like him, the same eyes that sparkled when she smiled. Robbie was gone and she had to forget him, but her grief returned as she watched his daughter cross the stage carrying herself the same way her father had, with the same set to her shoulders, the same black hair curling around her face. Diana cried.

Fred never recovered from his bout of influenza, and he died after developing pneumonia. The funeral was held at the First Baptist Church. Not many folks attended, but her cousin Jane was there. Jane was the one who had introduced Diana to Fred all those years ago.

That day Cassie wondered why her father even went to that church. He certainly didn't adhere to their Christian beliefs.

After the burial, Cassie walked to the parking lot with Jane's daughter, Andrea. "You know," she confided, "I just can't feel sorry that he's gone. I really don't feel a thing. I never did. The man seemed like a stranger. He never felt like a father to me."

"Well, that's because he *wasn't* your father." Andrea smirked. "Mama told me years ago, claimed it was a secret, so I never said anything. Guess it doesn't matter, now that he's dead."

That night Cassie told her mother what Andrea had said.

"Don't pay any attention to Andrea," Diana said. "She always did have a vivid imagination. Just put it out of your mind."

Cassie did put it out of her mind for quite a while, but the question arose again when she married her high school sweetheart, Bo, who was a blue-eyed blond. Their baby, precious little Ellen, was born with very dark skin and coal black hair. Bo had questions that Cassie couldn't answer, and soon he filed for divorce.

After Fred's death, Diana sold the farm and bought a little house in town. She was promoted to director of the program for poor mothers, which paid her enough to live on. Cassie and Ellen moved in with her.

Ellen learned to walk early, but walking was a waste of time to a little girl who was born with happy feet. When she was three, her mother enrolled her in dancing classes.

Yet somehow Cassie never forgot what Andrea said about Fred not being her father. She knew her mother was keeping a secret, so she asked again who her father was.

This time she got an answer. "I'm so sorry, Cassie, I have lied long enough. Your father's name was Robbie Davis. I met him at the Red Cross canteen when I was a volunteer. He was a private in the army, and I loved him very much."

Cassie was stunned. "Mama, if I'm not Fred Lewis' daughter, I need to know who the hell I am!"

"Of course, you deserve the truth, but I think Robbie was killed in Vietnam. We both need to know what really happened to him."

Soon after that, Diana bought a subscription to Ancestry.com and spent weeks taking computer classes. Then, late one night when she felt ready and the house was quiet, she got on Ancestry and clicked on *Search*. She entered Robert Davis, born in Dixon, North Carolina on July 25, 1944. Then she entered, Pvt. in US army, served in Vietnam.

That was all she knew about him. Her hand trembled when she hit *Enter*. Her heart raced as she waited to see what turned up. She expected to see …. died in combat on…. buried in …. Instead, she saw: Chaplin in VA hospital, Richmond, Va.

She couldn't believe her eyes. He was alive! She began shaking. She wanted to scream with joy, to awaken Cassie. *No,* she told herself, *he probably has a family—a wife and children.*

Diana wrote down the hospital address and gave it to Cassie the next morning. "I'm sure he's made a life for himself. It would be a horrible intrusion for me to contact him."

But Cassie said, "Well, *I'm* going to contact him. He may have a wife and children, but he left a daughter behind, and I'm going to tell him so!" She sent a letter to Chaplin Robert Davis in care of the VA hospital in Richmond, VA, and in a few days she received a reply.

Dear Cassie,

I am so very happy to hear from you, and I want to meet you as soon as possible. To answer your question about my family – I have none. I was married once. It only lasted a short time. I would like to see your mother again, too. May I come for a visit? I anxiously await your reply.

Cassie waited at gate 15 for the passengers to arrive on United Airlines 756 from Richmond, Virginia. Chaplin Davis was the last person to come through the gate – a tall, handsome, dark-skinned man. His hair, white now, was pulled back into a pony tail. A gold chain with a cross hung around his neck.

He came toward her leaning heavily on a cane and dragging his left leg. He looked into the face that so resembled his own and into dark brown eyes that matched his. "It's really you!" he cried, "My dear Cassie!"

"How can you tell?" She teased, because seeing him was like looking into a mirror.

"There's no doubt at all." He smiled and hugged her to him "Thank God."

Cassie took her father to dinner at a local restaurant, where he asked questions about her and Diana faster than she could answer.

But there was one thing she did not tell him. They were almost to Ellen's dance recital, before she told him she had a surprise.

The curtain rose, the music began, and a group of little ballerinas danced their way onto the stage. Cassie leaned close to her father and whispered, "The third girl in the front row, with dark black curls and dark skin, the one in the pink tutu—that's your granddaughter, Ellen."

"Oh, my God!" he gasped so loud, people turned around to look.

Robbie Davis would have one more surprise that night—the yellow ribbon Diana had tied around the tree by her front door: *if you still want me, tie a yellow ribbon round the ole oak tree.*

Ellen ran into the house squealing, "We found my granddaddy! We found him! He came to see me dance."

Robbie was nervous, but he managed a polite: "Hello, Diana. I hope this isn't a terrible inconvenience."

Diana fought back tears when she saw her beloved. "We've been looking forward to this," she shyly began. "You're looking well Robbie. It's been a very long time."

"Yes, it sure has." His big hand trembled when he took Diana's.

"We'll give you two some time to catch up," Cassie interrupted. "I'll take Ellen upstairs for a bath, then we'll come down and say goodnight."

Diana placed another log on the fire and picked up her knitting. "I thought you were dead." She struggled to keep the emotion out of her voice.

"I *almost* died," he told her. "I was wounded shortly after I arrived in Vietnam. I was in intensive care for some time, and then transferred to another hospital, where the doctors worked for months trying to save my leg. Well, I still have that leg, what's left of it, and I'm thankful for that. Eventually I went to Walter Reed for rehab.

"As soon as I could get around with a cane, I attended college on the GI Bill, then on to Divinity School…"

He paused and stared at her as the fire crackled and the seconds ticked on the mantle clock. Diana waited, torn between wanting to hug him or hate him for leaving her.

Finally, he cleared his throat and continued, his speech. "Diana, please try to understand. Growing up as a mixed-race child was hard. I didn't fit in anywhere, and neither race really wanted me. That's how it was back then. I always promised myself that I would never give that legacy to a child. But I was young and reckless when we met and crazy in love. The hardship I caused you is unforgivable, and I'm so very sorry."

"Don't be sorry for Cassie. She was a blessing. But it's too bad she had to grow up without you. When I finally told her the truth about us, she was determined to find her daddy."

Just then Ellen, wearing pajamas and clutching her doll, danced into the room and climbed into her grandfather's lap. "Will you tell me a story, Granddaddy?"

"I will indeed," he chuckled. Ellen hugged her doll and snuggled in his arms. "Once upon a time there were three little pigs," he said in a very soft, slow voice. Ellen listened intently, and as the story went on, her eyelids got heavier and heavier until they closed.

"The pigs' mama didn't have enough food for them all," he continued, his voice becoming even softer and slower, "so she sent them out into the world. The first little pig built a house of straw, and the second one built a house of ….."

Robbie's voice got slower and slower and the room got quieter and quieter until all you could hear was the clock ticking on the mantle and Robbie's soft snoring.

Diana got up and threw another log on the fire. It crackled and popped, sending sparks up the chimney and heat into the room.

She smiled and whispered when Cassie came into the room, "God only knows how long it would have taken him to get to the wolf

43

huffing and puffing. You should go to bed, Cassie. I'll take care of Sleeping Beauty and Prince Charming."

Robbie snored softly, his head resting against his granddaughter's curly black hair. The big bad wolf was not coming to blow Diana's house down—not tonight—and for the first time in a very long time, she felt at peace. She kissed them both, covered them with a blanket and turned out the light.

EMILY

Before she knew it, she was being dragged by the hair behind the gym. The basketball game had just ended. He had scored 18 points, the star player on the home team. She was one of the cheerleaders who had cheered him on.

His hand was over her mouth, she tried to scream but a muted squeak was all she could manage. He threw her on the ground, pushed his hand underneath her blue cheer leading skirt, pulled down the matching pants and growled in her ear, "I'll make you sorry you didn't go out with me, you conceited bitch."

Emily had bruises on her back and legs and a bloody nose when she got home. She was terrified and sobbing hysterically when she told her parents what had happened.

"If you'd come right home like I told you, this wouldn't have happened," her father yelled as he pulled off his belt, threw her on the floor and slashed her across her bottom.

It was two months after graduation when she began to show. She was sent to Aunt Josephine's to have the baby. New York was like the other side of the world to Emily Morris, but it became her home. Aunt Josephine, Uncle Antonio Costello and their mentally handicapped daughter, Lucinda, became her family.

The baby was a girl. Emily named her Katherine Costello after her favorite actress, Katherine Hepburn. Emily got a job waiting tables in Uncle Antonio's restaurant, while Aunt Josephine took care of Lucinda and Katherine.

Antonio's was a favorite place for actors to gather after a show. Portraits of famous stars hung on the walls. The tables were covered with white tablecloths and each held a candle inside a glass globe that twinkled like fireflies on a dark night. A piano player and a singer performed *O Sole Mio, Santa Lucia, Torna a Sorriento* and other songs for the hungry customers who dined on fine Italian food.

Antonio's brother Theo, a flamboyant, openly gay man, who played Romeo in an off-Broadway performance of Romeo and Juliette, was a regular. His hair, dyed jet black, stood out in contrast to his calf length fox fur coat.

Theo entered Antonio's with the swagger of a glorified matinee idol, usually with Louisa Mayfield on his arm. Louisa had starred in several winning movies. Previously a strawberry blonde, she was now a sixty-year-old flaming redhead whose once milky white skin had taken on the appearance of crinkled paper. Louisa, who was several years older than Theo and several times divorced, was now a washed-up actress who used Theo as an escort. Together they made a rather handsome couple.

Theo, when dining at Antonio's, always asked to be seated at "Em's" table. And always Antonio would kiss his brother and Louisa on both cheeks, wink at his niece and whisper, "Free tiramisu tonight, sweetheart."

Theo gave Emily free tickets to the theater and she began going on her afternoon off. One of her favorite places was the Ed Sullivan Theater, where she saw *Hello Dolly, Oklahoma, Sunset Boulevard* and other wonderful shows.

When Em was promoted to hostess, the charming young lady greeted many guests by name, making them feel welcome. And as Antonio aged, he began to depend more and more on his niece.

Uncle Theo, who loved children, especially little Katherine, delighted in taking her to matinees, ice skating in Rockefeller Center, Christmas Shopping and having her photo made with Santa.

Uncle "T", as Katherine called him, adored entertaining in his 63rd street apartment, which was decorated as flamboyantly as Theo himself. His cook served the best wines and the most delightful meals on Theo's Raffaellesco blue china from Tuscany.

Every room in his apartment held vases of flowers, usually roses, his favorites. He owned huge mirrors, heavy rose-colored drapes and expensive antique furniture placed on plush rugs purchased during his many trips to Italy to visit cousins.

Theo Costello welcomed his guests dressed in a silk lounge outfit and flashing a large diamond ring on his right hand. He kissed his guests on both cheeks, except the giggling little Katherine, whom he lifted in his arms and swung around his lavish rooms shouting, "Bellissimo angioletto!"

One July night was extremely hot in the city. When the Broadway performances ended and and people poured from the theaters looking for a place to have a cocktail and a good meal, Antonio's filled up fast. The air conditioning was running at full speed, the wait staff and kitchen staff were going mad trying to keep up, and the special, lobster ravioli with tomato vodka sauce, was running low.

Em was seating people as fast as she could when one of the kitchen staff approached, his face white as pizza dough. "We need you in the kitchen, hurry!"

She wiped the perspiration from her neck and headed through the swinging doors. The young man said, "He's out there, on the loading dock. He needed air."

Antonio was lying on a bench, his shirt collar open. One of the cooks was fanning him with a menu. Emily dialed 911 and rode with him to the hospital.

The stroke left Antonio with paralysis on his right side and slurred speech. When he came home from the hospital, he was one more person for her aunt to care for. When Emily began looking for a nurse to help, she realized that not only was something wrong with her uncle, but also with his finances.

She questioned his bookkeeper, who was initially reluctant to give her any information. Finally, he showed her the list of unpaid bills and bank loans.

She confided in Uncle Theo, who said, "Antonio was always a poor manager, my darling Em. Give me some time to think it through, and then I'll try to offer a suggestion."

But Theo was not a money manager, either. He was an actor who belonged on the stage in front of adoring audiences. He understood standing ovations, curtain calls and escorting Louisa around to shine among the stars.

Lucinda, Antonio's handicapped daughter, was getting worse, having one epileptic attack after the other, Uncle Antonio was failing fast and Aunt Jo, even with a nurse to help, was overwhelmed.

So Em ran the restaurant and tried her best to pay the bills. Uncle Theo did his part by lending support and treating the cast to drinks after the show. The actors usually ordered several drinks and dinner, resulting in the restaurant having a good night now and then, yet it was all Em could do to keep the doors open.

One night, in his sleep, Antonio's heart stopped. After a private funeral in St. Michael's Catholic Church, everyone was invited to join the family for lunch in Theo's apartment. That's where Emily met tall, handsome, blue-eyed Clark Mayfield, Louisa's son by her third husband.

His smile was irresistible when he put his arm around Emily's waist and pulled her aside to tell her that he had a business proposition to discuss.

When they met the next day, Clark explained his plan: a tour company called *Mayfield Tour's*. He would advertise the tours throughout the country, pick the people up at the airport in a tour bus, provide three nights in a hotel, two plays and on their last night they would dine at Antonio's.

Several months into the plan, Em began making a dent in the bills. Each night she set aside a special table for Uncle Theo, Aunt Jo, Louisa, Katherine and Clark. They all loved eating at the restaurant amid all the hustle and bustle.

But then one night Clark did not show up. When the after-theater crowd came in, instead of the usual light-hearted laughter, they were solemn and subdued, and soon Emily knew why. A plane had skidded off a La Guardia runway and crashed. It was all over the news.

Clark Mayfield was on that plane. There had been two fatalities and serious injuries.

Louisa was hysterical. Theo took her home, promising to locate her son. He called every hospital in the city. Hours later, he located Clark, who had a concussion, facial cuts, a collapsed lung and a broken leg.

Emily visited Clark in the hospital every day before going to the restaurant. At first, he was reluctant to let her see the scars on his face, but Emily Morris was a woman who did not take no for an answer.

Louisa was still too hysterical to be of much help, so Emily discussed plastic surgery with his doctors. She learned that Clark's concussion was no longer a danger, his lung was healing, and his leg was stabilized. He could be released, if he had the proper care. The nurse she had employed when Uncle Antonio was sick was still caring for Lucinda, so Emily took Clark home with her.

Mayfield Tours employees kept the business afloat until Clark was back on his feet and able return to his own house. But when the time came to leave, he would not go without Emily.

Together they made Mayfield Tours and Antonio's a huge success. Theo got the leading role in a Neil Simon play, and Louisa was hired for a bit part. After their performances ended each night, more theater goers than ever made their way to the famous Antonio's for dinner.

Wonderful smells emanated from the kitchen each time a waiter rushed through the swinging doors bringing a tray of delicious food. Candles twinkled on every table as a soloist sang *That's Amore*.

Hanging on the back wall near the kitchen was a portrait of the founder, Antonio Costello, and beneath the portrait was a table reserved for his devoted family: Josephine, Theo, Louisa, Katherine, his niece Emily and her husband Clark Mayfield.

Sometimes when Emily glanced at her uncle's portrait, she could swear he winked at her and whispered, *well done, sweetheart.*

FAITH

Fantastic was the word that flashed through Phillip's mind as he said goodnight to the President of the Republic and other dignities. It truly had been a wonderful evening and a delicious meal. He had to find Faith and thank her.

Phillip Keener knew very little about the West African country when he accepted the ambassadorship. Faith, a native, had been chef at the embassy for several years and once again she had saved the day.

He didn't know what he would have done without her tutelage. Soon he would have to tell her that he was leaving, but not tonight. He found her in the kitchen directing the clean-up.

She wiped perspiration from her face, brushed her hands across her apron and smiled when he came in. "How was the meal sir?"

"Fantastic!" He beamed. "They enjoyed it immensely, especially your chicken and peanut casserole. I thought His Honor might make himself sick he ate so much."

"Oh, never mind him, Mr. Keener. His Honor's body has become used to his over indulgences."

"Faith, I need to have a little chat with you. Maybe tomorrow right after breakfast."

Oh no, she thought. *I have displeased him. I am in trouble.*

After she served Mr. Keener's breakfast, he asked her to sit and have coffee with him, and then in his usual quiet manner he said, "I am leaving. I have finally accepted that I was not meant to be an ambassador. I want to be a teacher. My heart is in the classroom and I have accepted a job back in the States. I'll be a teaching in a small town called Dixon, North Carolina."

Faith was speechless. Her heart almost stopped.

"I would like for you to come with me and go to an accredited culinary school. You would have to get an American GED first, but that would be no problem. Then with a degree from accredited culinary school, you could make a lot more money. You don't have to give me an answer now. Just think it over."

"You very kind to me, sir, but no, I will not go. I am cooking to please the Lord. The missionaries tell me it is God's will, and I must do it or God will be very displeased with me."

"But if cooking is not where your heart is, what is it you want to do?"

"Oh, I want to do nursing, in a hospital, sir. It was always in my heart. I want to care for the sick, but I must obey the Lord."

"Faith, the missionaries are paid by their church to preach to you about God. They were sent here by the Baptist church to teach you. But they don't know what is in your heart. You are the only one who knows what that is. It seems we both must listen to our hearts and follow our own paths.

"But I have a son, Malaki."

"And your husband?"

"Gone, sir, with another woman."

"Malaki will be able to get a good education, and you can go to nursing school. I will see that you both have what you need. I have no family of my own and I have rented a large house off campus. You and your son will have the whole upstairs. Your job will be to run the house for me, and to go to school.

"I know this is a big decision Faith. It takes a strong woman to undertake such a challenge, but I have confidence in you."

It was a terrifying decision indeed for a woman who had grown up in a family compound, living in a simple hut surrounded by the huts of family members. She and her siblings walked miles to get water. Electricity, their only luxury, came on and off at will.

When Faith's parents had enough money, she went to school. Now it took all she could earn to send her own child.

She decided there was only one correct decision.

***

The flight was terrifying. Every time the plane bumped, Faith believed God was showing displeasure with her. She closed her eyes, gripped the seat handles and prayed for God to forgive her for what she was doing.

She was sick to her stomach and trembling uncontrollably when she entered the Charlotte airport. She held on to Malaki for fear she would lose him among the crowds of people that rushed past.

Then a nice-looking man with curly blond hair approached them, threw his arms around Phillip and said, "Thank God you're home, Flip. How was your flight, love?"

"The flight was long and a little bumpy, so we're exhausted. It's so good to be home, Pete."

Peter Austell hugged Faith and shook Malaki's hand. "Welcome to North Carolina, my friends."

Malaki froze in awe of the yellow convertible that Peter put them in to make the trip up the interstate to a big white house on a tree-lined street in Dixon—their new home.

Phillip showed Faith the awesome kitchen where she would learn to cook American food. It had all the running water she needed, a refrigerator that made ice and enough electricity to run two ovens.

Her shy little boy made another awesome discovery—the baby grand piano in the far corner of the living room. "It's okay, Mali, check it out," Peter told him. When Maliki brushed his little brown fingers across the ivory keys, his face beamed with joy.

Malaki's head was swimming with all the new things he had been exposed to, but there was one more treat in store for the tired little boy from Ghana, and that was the Lancaster's barbeque and hushpuppies that Peter warmed up for their dinner.

While Phillip was teaching Faith how to prepare American dishes, Peter was buying her son American clothes—his first pair of jeans, just like Peter's, and a book bag like the other kids carried to school. He got a haircut at the barbershop on Main Street and ice cream at the Soda Shop.

Peter, who was the band director at Mali's school, began giving the little boy piano lessons after classes. Nearly every Saturday the two of them had lunch at Lancaster's.

Soon, almost every afternoon after school, Mali could be heard playing beginning pieces on the piano and Peter asking, "Did you practice like I told you? Well, do that again. You're missing the middle part. Mali, do the scales again."

"I can't do it."

"Yes, you can. Concentrate."

Faith and her son began attending the Baptist church. The minister welcomed her and asked her to become a member, but when he learned that she lived with Peter and Phillip, the intolerant man explained that she lived in a house of sin and that she should move her son to a more suitable environment. He also explained that he could authorize money from the foreign mission's fund to pay their airfare back home, and advised that she should go as soon as possible.

Faith was terribly confused. She had displeased the Lord. The minister had told her as much. She must take her son and go home, but Malaki was so happy. He loved his piano lessons and he loved Peter, who was like a father to him. She would pray. The Lord always answered her prayers.

That same afternoon an excited Peter explained that he needed her help. "Faith, Flip's birthday is next week. I'm having a party and inviting some of his friends from the college. I want you to cook an authentic African meal like you cooked for him at the embassy."

Peter decorated the house with balloons, paper streamers and birthday banners. Ten of Phillip's fellow professors arrived for the Ghanaian meal consisting of tomato stew with okra, pumpkin seeds served with rice, octopus, fontom and tea bread.

Faith looked like she had stepped out of a National Geographic magazine in her dress of gold, red, lime and cobalt blue with a cobalt head wrap. Malaki wore a traditional Ghanaian male smock and surprised everyone by playing happy birthday on the baby grand.

When Mali's lessons had advanced beyond Peter's ability, he arranged for a teacher at the college to give him more advanced instruction.

Worrying that her son was becoming hopelessly attached, Faith decided to visit the Baptist minister again and take him up on his offer to fly her back to Ghana. She was planning to see him as soon as she finished the breakfast dishes. She was emptying the dishwasher when Phillip came in and said, "Get your coat Faith, I have a surprise for you."

It was a little blue Volkswagen bug. "It's all yours," he said. "The title is in your name. Get in. I'll teach you how to drive."

Faith loved the little blue bug and happily drove it to her school, where she was training to become a nurse. She would definitely go home once she was certified. But then, since Malaki had one more year in high school, she took a job in the local hospital until he graduated.

Peter had applied for several scholarships for Malaki, and just before his graduation, her son got some surprising news. His interest in classical music and his expertise in Beethoven had earned him a scholarship to Julliard.

For his graduation present, Peter gave Malaki his yellow convertible and bought him everything he needed for life in New York.

The house was so quiet once Malaki was gone. Faith missed him terribly. Phillip and Peter were spending more time together. Now it was time to go home. She sent her resume to two hospitals in Ghana.

It was pouring down rain one afternoon when Faith came in from work to make spaghetti for Phillip and Peter and found them toasting each other with champagne. Peter exclaimed, "Flip and I are getting married! Can you believe it? The Unitarian minister has agreed to perform the ceremony. It's really going to happen—in June!

"We want you to bake a fabulous wedding cake and plan the reception, Faith. Mali will play our wedding music. We will invite as many friends as the house will hold."

After all they had done, how could she refuse?

Three weeks before the wedding, Faith was at work when she was called to the emergency room. She found Peter there, crying. "They think Flip's had a stroke," he sobbed.

Phillip Keener was partially paralyzed and required a lot of assistance. Peter told Faith that he was planning to hire a nurse to care for him.

"No sir, you will not. He has a nurse."

Several months later, the house smelled like a garden of roses. Tall, handsome, composed Malaki, dressed in a tuxedo strolled in. He gracefully lifted the tail of his tux and took his place at the baby grand. He played Beethoven's Moonlight Sonata, and then the wedding march. Peter entered pushing Phillip's wheelchair.

After their honeymoon, sun streamed through the kitchen window and Phillip watched Faith making Mali's favorite meatloaf recipe. Mali had finished a concert tour and was driving down from New York for a long break.

"Mr. Phillip, you know Mali is living with a girl, don't you?" Faith asked. "She's a *white* girl."

"Good Lord, Faith. Does your Baptist preacher know about this?"

"Blessed Jesus, no! That man is in a nursing home now. No need for him to know about that."

Faith had finished making a salad and was peeling potatoes when Peter rushed in all out of breath. "Mali just called on my cell phone. He'll be here any minute."

Peter was pacing back and forth, looking at his watch when they heard a car pull into the driveway. He ran to the window and pulled back the curtain. "He's here!" Peter yelled as he ran out the door. "My God, the wee little bastard is driving a brand-new yellow convertible!"

"How many miles you got on it, Mali?" Peter was asking as they came."

"Just over a thousand," Mali answered.

"Take care of it. Don't forget to change the oil regularly," Peter instructed.

"Yes, sir, I know about changing the oil. Remember, you used to make me do it to your car *and* wash it *and* wax it *and* put air in the tires."

Malaki had let his hair grow. It was pulled back into a ponytail. He was wearing a colorful plaid shirt tucked into tight fitting jeans. Faith hardly recognized the handsome young man who kissed her and said, "I missed you, Ma Ma!

"Is that meatloaf I smell, Ma Ma? Oh, Ma Ma, I have so much to tell you."

"Sit, Mali," Peter said. "And try to calm down while I get you a glass of wine."

"Now Mali, tell us about your tour. What did the audiences like most?"

"Oh, Beethoven's Piano Concerto No. 5. It brought the audiences to their feet every time. I brought a video so you can see for yourself."

"That must have made you happy," Phillip said.

"That is very true sir, but always my heart was here. I dreamed the whole time about coming home."

"Home is where the heart is," Peter added, "where they love you the most and feed you the best." He raised a glass of wine. "Well done, son, welcome home."

JANIE

Clyde Sides was a train engineer for Southern Railway in Spencer. Janie met him at the Dixon Soda Shop. He had the week of July 4th off and had come to Dixon to visit a cousin before making his weekly trip to Asheville.

Janie Cashion had just turned 18. Her family owned Cashion's Funeral Parlor just down the street. They lived upstairs over the funeral parlor, which was hot as an oven in the Carolina heat. She had come to the soda shop to cool off and get an ice-cold lemonade.

Clyde Sides never passed up a chance to flirt with a pretty girl. He winked at Janie and motioned for her to come sit beside him.

Janie lived above a room full of caskets, dead bodies, smells of embalming fluid and sad, grieving family members. Laughter was not allowed—ever. Her spirit felt as dead as the bodies her father embalmed. Her 18-year-old soul longed to live, laugh, listen to beautiful music and dance in the arms of a handsome young man.

She was looking for a ticket out of Dixon, so when Clyde's arm brushed against her, she tingled with excitement.

After a brief courtship, they married and lived in a wretched apartment house in Spencer with eight other families, sharing one bathroom between the four of them. Janie had to get used to screaming children, crying babies and yelling mothers.

It was a far cry from the quiet little college town where she grew up. Now she heard loud locomotives spewing steam, shrill train whistles and box cars banging into each other all hours of the night. She breathed air filled with smoke and cinders, she always felt dirty, and the husband she hardly knew barely noticed her.

Clyde left early one morning to make his usual run to Asheville and would be away for a week. She was cleaning the kitchen when someone knocked on her door. It was Clyde's boss.

With a serious look on his face, he informed her that a switchman in a nearby town had forgotten to pull the proper switch and Clyde's passenger train and a freight train loaded with grain had collided. He needed to know where she wanted her husband's body sent

Clyde didn't have any next of kin, or none that he ever told her about. She asked them to send the body to Cashion's Funeral Parlor in Dixon and to take her with it. Everything she owned fit into the small suitcase she carried when she boarded the train to Dixon with Clyde's body onboard. Southern Railway gave her barely enough money to pay his funeral expenses.

Her father, as pompous and disdainful as ever, met her at the station, loaded the body into his hearse and headed to the funeral parlor.

When they arrived, Grant Gifford was delivering one of the caskets he made in his basement. The plain pine casket didn't even have a lining, but it was all she could afford.

Grant's pleasant smile and kind, sympathetic eyes met hers and he said the first consoling words that anyone had uttered to her; "I'm so sorry for your loss Mrs. Sides. Is there anything I can do?"

"Well, I guess I'll be looking for a place to live," she said, "if you know any anything."

"There is a little house next door to me that's available to rent," he answered.

It was small, but all she needed. She paid the first month's rent with enough left over to buy a sewing machine.

Grant promised to spread word around that she took in sewing. Soon the folks at Dixon College, Johnny Brown at Johnny Brown's Department Store, Rush Williams at William's Men's Clothing store and Frank Johnson at Johnson's Dry Cleaners were all giving Janie work.

Janie asked Grant if he would like her to make satin linings for his caskets. A joyful smile crossed his lips, and in a quiet, emotional voice he managed to utter a simple, "Oh yes."

After Janie was settled in her little house, she went next door to meet Grant's wife and realized immediately that being neighborly was not Bessie Gifford's strong suit. The big woman shuffled to the door in her battered black bedroom slippers and with an almost homicidal look said, "What do you want?"

A teenager named Millie lived right behind Janie. She was one of the only black folks living on that side of town. Millie had been in the creek bottom picking blackberries when she saw Janie going to Bessie's. She knew it wouldn't go well because she and everyone in Dixon knew that Bessie Gifford was mean as a snake.

"Well, bless your heart, honey," Janie said when Millie showed up at her door with a quart of blackberries. "That's mighty sweet of you. I'll bake us a cobbler. You come back tomorrow and have some with me."

That same night, it was pitch dark when Janie heard men on horseback come galloping through her yard. She couldn't tell who they were, because they wore white sheets. They headed straight to Millie's house. One man carried a torch that lit up the whole yard. They galloped around the front of Millie's house throwing rocks. One of them smashed through her front window.

Janie watched from her kitchen as Millie led her two little sisters to the back porch, where they climbed up to a low flat place on the roof. The tin roof, still hot from the afternoon sun, must have burned their hands and knees until they reached a blanket hidden under the eaves beneath low hanging branches.

Janie grabbed the shotgun she kept hidden behind the door, ran outside and fired a shot into the air. "Which one of you assholes wants a bullet in your backside?" she yelled.

She fired off another shot before the revolting monsters turned their horses and started down the hill behind her house. Janie ran to the frightened girls and coaxed them down from their hiding place.

The terrified little girls were crying and trembling with fear. Millie was more worried about what her mother would say about her torn dress. But Janie was fuming about the unconcerned parents who went out partying and left their children home alone.

She consoled the children as best she could, fixed them a dish of blackberry cobbler and made them a pallet on the kitchen floor

The sun was just peeking over the eastern edge of Dixon when Janie Sides heard Masie, the children's mother, call for Millie. "Where are you girl? I told you not to leave this house. You gonna get a whippin' you won't never forget!"

Janie Cashion Sides marched herself over to Masie's and blessed her out for leaving the girls alone. She threatened to call the police if she ever did it again.

That afternoon, Janie finished sewing a white satin lining for Grant and yelled for him to meet her at the fence. The quilted lining had a soft, cotton filled pillow with little white ribbon streamers attached. Tears came to Grant's eyes when he saw it, and it took a few minutes before he could manage a grateful, "Thank you, Janie."

His wife, Bessie, was watching them from her bedroom window. Janie could see her spiteful, accusatory face behind the lace curtains.

When she asked Grant about his wife's sour attitude, he confided that Bessie had been "seeing things". She had accused him of burying bodies under their front porch. The dead people, she claimed, would come out at night and sing and dance around a tree in the front yard.

"You best be careful, Grant," Janie warned him. "Maybe you need to go talk to Dr. Forrest about Bessie?"

***

Janie owned a pecan tree, so she decided to bake a pie. She asked Millie to come over to pick up some nuts. The child had almost finished, when Janie saw the hooded men coming on horseback, their sheets flapping in the breeze. Millie dropped the bucket, climbed up the tree and hid in the branches.

There were five men in all. One pounded a cross in front of Millie's house. One on a black horse poured gasoline on the cross, while another held a torch to the cross. Janie heard a loud swish as flames flashed against the dark shy and the fiery cross sputtered and crackled, sending off a cloud of black smoke.

Next shots rang out into the sky as Janie Sides shouted, "Get away from here before I kill somebody!"

The shots not only scared the men, they also caused a flock of birds to explode from the tree where Millie was hiding. She yelled "Oh, good God Almighty, Miss Janie, don't kill nobody!"

When the men had gone, Janie helped Millie down from the tree. "Don't worry about me killing nobody. I couldn't hit the broad side of a cow barn. Now you come inside and let me get you calmed down and fix you some cornbread and milk."

It took a while before the child stopped trembling enough to crumble her cornbread into the glass of cold milk, and then she said, "There weren't any chitlins in the cornbread. You forgot the chitlins, Miss Janie?"

"Well, no, I didn't Millie, God created chitlins for a purpose and it ain't got nothin to do with cornbread."

Later that week, Janie saw Grant walking to his little Ford pickup truck. He was limping. He had a bruise on his cheek and a black eye. "What happened to you?" she asked.

"Just a little accident."

"Well, what kind of accident?" Janie knew Bessie was behind the lace curtains watching them.

"Well, I ran into a broom."

"You can't run into a broom, Grant. Not unless somebody is swinging it. You're hurt and you're going to see Dr. Forrest. Either you tell him what happened, or I'll go to the police and ask them to investigate."

Grant did go to Dr. Forrest, and Dr. Forrest told the police that Bessie Gifford was crazy. Soon Grant's wife was in a mental hospital.

With Bessie gone and Millie's family moving across town, the neighborhood became quiet and uneventful. Grant continued making caskets in his basement workshop, and Janie continued making beautiful quilted satin linings for him.

But then things changed.

Grant put a gate in the fence beneath Bessie's bedroom window and created a path leading right up to Janie's kitchen door. Almost every night he followed his nose to the delicious smells coming from her kitchen. Often she made southern fried chicken to go with potatoes and gravy. Janie had whipped cream to go on the apple pie still warm from the oven and always a pot of freshly perked coffee on the stove.

And the table was always set for two.

KASIE

"Miss Clark? This is Steven from the plant. We found your brother's body in the lake this morning. So sorry for the bad news. Miss Clark, can you hear me? This is a bad connection. Miss Clark, are you all right? Shall I send someone for you?"

It was 26 degrees and snowing in Boone. The 8:00 AM school bell had just rung. Noisy kids dressed in heavy coats and wearing boots were taking their seats when Kasie got the call.

Their assignment had been to finish reading *To Kill a Mocking Bird* and write a paper characterizing Scout—what kind of person was she, and what was her importance in the family dynamics?

Kasie had been looking forward to reading their reports when she got the call about her brother. It was a shock, although Kasie and he never got along. George had little use for women except to meet his needs. They were almost subhuman to him. But suicide? Why on earth would he do that?

George took over the family business, Clark's Yarn Mill, after their father's death. George Clark, Sr. founded the company in the 1940's and left it to them jointly, but her brother had excluded her, a mere woman, from any part of it.

Kasie didn't know her sister-in-law very well. She knew they had two small children and that was about all.

Well, she would have to go home, but in this weather, how could she get down the mountain? A taxi had chains. That was her only hope.

When she reached her brother's house and rang the bell, a little boy about five came to the door. "Are you Georgie?" she asked. "I'm your Aunt Kasie, may I come in? Where is your mother?"

"Mama's in bed upstairs," he said.

Kasie started up the stairs as a little girl still dressed in pajamas was coming down. "Hi, sweetheart," Kasie said, "will you show me where your mama is?"

"Sandy, I'm Kasie," she said to the huge lump hidden under a quilt. "I'm so sorry about George, and I'm here to help in any way I can. Please tell me what I can do."

Sandy threw the cover back and yelled, "Why did that son-of-a-bitch have to go jump in the damn lake? Sure, he had problems. He was in trouble, I knew that. But he had a family to take care of. But to go and jump in the lake, what the hell!"

When Sandy Clark struggled to sit up, Kasie saw that she was very pregnant. "What can *I* do?" Kasie asked.

"Feed the kids. Georgie said we're out of cereal."

"I'll take them to McDonald's. What can I bring you?"

"Nothing, damn it! I can't keep anything down." She groaned, lay back down and pulled the quilt over her head.

Kasie was straightening up the house when the doorbell rang. It was a man from the funeral home. "We were wondering if maybe a family member could meet with us tomorrow and help with some arrangements?"

"Yes. Of course. I am George's sister. His wife and I will be there." But when she asked Sandy about a funeral, Sandy shouted, "Funeral, hell. Cremate the son-of-a-bitch and spread his ashes on his secretary's desk."

Sandy went into premature labor that night. Her little girl was stillborn.

Steven from the plant called to inquire about funeral arrangements. "We aren't having a funeral," Kasie told him.

"Oh, well then, I'll just close for a couple of days out of respect. Can Mrs. Clark come down later and give us some direction?"

"I suppose I am the only family member who can do that, but I've got my hands full here. Can you manage for a few days?"

Sandy was depressed, grieving, mad as hell and basically a basket case. Her doctor gave her some tranquilizers and told her to stay in bed and rest.

The kids were confused, hungry, wondering when their daddy would be back and why their mother didn't get out of bed. Who was going make their meals, help them with baths and take Georgie to preschool? Besides all this, Kasie's principal kept calling demanding to know when she would be back.

So, it was a relief when Kasie got everyone fed, bathed and Georgie off to preschool. Then she could fix her hair, put on makeup, dress in the little black suit that she had meant to wear to the funeral and head down to Clark's Yarn Mill.

Steven Long was experiencing his own set of frustrations – questions from employees and newspaper reporters about why George

Clark took his own life. They asked if the mill was going to close, were paychecks going to be on time, when were orders going to be delivered and when were suppliers going to be paid?

Steven, George's longtime assistant, was in his office on the phone with a newspaper reporter when Kasie knocked. "Come in," he yelled, and then back into the phone, "No, I don't have any more to say about that now. Maybe later, goodbye."

He hung up and turned to the woman before him whose little black suit fit her like a glove. She wore a single strand of pearls and matching earrings. She held out her hand, "I'm Kasie Clark, Mr. Long."

"I'm sorry for your loss, Miss Clark," he said as he closed the door, shutting out the noise of spinning machines and loud voices.

Steven watched as she crossed her shapely legs and settled into the chair he had pulled out for her. Then he sought her full attention, speaking in a low, almost secretive voice. "I'll catch you up on things as best I can. I suppose you remember the layout of the mill and all about the spinning process. You can ask questions as we go along…

"Everyone is asking why your brother did what he did. I can probably fill in most of the blanks. Much of it will be unpleasant. Shall I start?"

"Start, Mr. Long."

"Your brother had been involved with his secretary, Janice Young, for years. Miss Young had his child about one year ago. After a long fight and with the help of her lawyer, she was awarded child support – quite a lot of child support—and maybe some hush money too.

"Besides that added expense, he was being sued by suppliers for money owed them, clients for undelivered merchandise and by banks for nonpayment of loans."

"I think I get the picture, Mr. Long. Not a pretty one, is it?"

"We are in a dire situation, Miss Clark, and if we don't find a way out soon, we will have to close the doors.

"Janice and I are the only ones who know the whole story. All of George's correspondence crossed her desk. She overheard all his phone calls and feels her importance here. To be honest, she had George over a barrel.

"I suppose you'll have to meet her sooner or later, but first let's take a tour and get you reacquainted with the business."

They went from the scouring department to picking and carding. In the dye area, the cotton was transformed into magical colors. Then it moved on to the spinning frames, where it was wound onto cones ready for shipping.

Kasie went home that afternoon, her head still spinning from all the noise, to find Sandy in bed and the children watching TV. She made a chicken and rice casserole for dinner and tried to imagine what help she could offer Steven.

The next morning, he took her into George's old office, shut the door and began pulling up accounts on the computer. He showed her which bills were outstanding and which businesses would cut them off if not paid soon.

Janice interrupted frequently, with telephone calls for either Steven or Kasie. She was eager to find out what was going on behind the closed doors. Kasie got the feeling that Steven didn't trust the woman, but he was very discreet.

After several days of discussions and Janice popping in and out pretending to need a file, Kasie was ready to offer a suggestion.

"Steven, besides the mill, our father left each of us money. I invested mine in stocks that should have increased in value. Also, I have a substantial 401K. If I cash these in, they would at least get us over this rough spot and we could begin anew. If we operate on a tight budget for a while, we could start making money again. And I think for sake of Clark Yarn Mill and everybody concerned, Janice Young must go. What do you think?"

"I think you won't get rid of her so easily. You'll have to pay her off."

"Oh, hell, I need a drink, Steven. Let's go somewhere and have dinner and see if we can come up with a plan."

They had ordered drinks and dinner when Steven asked, "So, you aren't going back to Boone?"

"Nope."

They had almost finished steak dinners when Steven's cell phone rang. "Oh, my God!" he said. "We'll be right there, Sam."

It's the night watchman," he explained. "The mills on fire!"

They could see the glow a block away. Two firetrucks and an ambulance were there. Ladders were raised over the left-wing, spraying water on the roof, and someone was being loaded into the ambulance.

"Stay here. Don't move," Steven said before disappearing inside.

Sparks were flying everywhere, and the heat was intense. The firemen were hosing down the main part of the plant to prevent the fire from spreading.

And then Sam came across the parking lot cradling a baby in his arms. "May I help you with that child?" Kasie asked.

"Well, I'd be pleased if you would, Miss Clark. It's Miss Janice's baby. I found her cryin' in Miss Janice's car. I finally got her calmed down and back to sleep. Been waitin' for Miss Janice to come out, but she ain't come yet. I'm beginnin' to wonder. There wasn't no reason for her to be there this time of night."

Kasie was sitting on a loading dock with the sleeping baby in her arms when it occurred to her that the child was her niece.

When the fire was finally under control, Steven came out the employee entrance soaking wet. "It was mostly limited to George's office and Janice's, some to mine," he said. "Janice's body was found in George's office. Apparently, she set the fire and accidently locked herself in. She was an angry woman, that's for sure, but this.....this is crazy.

"I'll take you and the child home," he added.

"To George's house? Oh no!" Kasie said. "Not with the baby. Sandy knows this baby is George's. Besides, she is grieving and terribly depressed over the loss of her own baby."

"You can spend the night at my apartment while you decide what to do, Kasie."

The next day Steven was busy with fire inspectors, police investigators, newspaper reporters and people from the insurance company.

Janice's landlady let Kasie into Janice's apartment to get some of the baby's things. "Oh, she led a very secluded life, Miss Clark. The only person who ever came here was Mr. Clark. Poor little Annalisa is not even a year old and already she's an orphan."

Kasie hired an older woman from the mill to babysit while she split her time between Annalisa, seeing to Sandy and helping Steven arrange for the fire-damaged wing to be rebuilt.

Steven made a space in a storage room for him and Kasie to work. He called in an accountant, who soon discovered that Janice had been embezzling money.

"That answers a lot of questions," Kasie said. "She set the fire to cover her tracks."

Steven managed to pull up all the info they needed on the computer to begin paying the bills.

The manufacturing part of the mill suffered only minor smoke damage, so the yarn manufacturing went on as usual. Together they began putting things in order.

Kasie got several new accounts – one of them was a Japanese company.

She and Annalisa stayed on in Steven's apartment while she looked for a small house to buy. He teased her about being a mama and he called her "Mama Kasie," so much so that Annalisa, who was just beginning to talk, began calling her Mama, too.

When Sandy finally decided to arise from her bed and rejoin the living, she started by joining a gym, losing weight, having a tummy tuck and joining an on-line dating service.

In a few short months Sandy was flying back and forth to California to see Mr. Walter Bucannon, a much older and very wealthy man. Soon she agreed to become the third Mrs. Bucannon. Wanting to put the painful past behind, she signed over her interest in Clark's Yarn Mill to Kasie and allowed her to assume the remainder of the loan on her house. Soon thereafter, Sandy Clark and her children were gone.

Annalisa got her own room when she and Kasie moved into Sandy and George's house. Annalisa had become so attached to Steven and he to her, that he spent most of his time there, too.

Kasie managed to get some of the old accounts to increase their orders. The Japanese doubled theirs and insisted she come to Japan and tour their facility.

A few weeks later, Kasie and Steven were seated on a 747 on the runway of the local airport. A stewardess instructed them about how to use the oxygen masks, secure the food trays, fasten their seatbelts and prepare for takeoff. The engines roared, the plane raced down the runway at a breathtaking speed and lifted off the ground. When they were safely above the clouds and in the calm blue sky, Steven Long finally relaxed, leaned over and kissed his bride.

LOUELLA

The leaves in the mountains around Flat Rock were in their most brilliant reds and yellows due to a cold, rainy September and a perfect October. Abe Martin had harvested his corn. The stalks stood in tall shocks around the split rail fence surrounding the pasture where his cows had just come from their morning milking.

Robert Stone, who grew up on a farm near the Martin's, emerged from the veils of morning mist and rounded the curve leading up to Abe's. He had left Dixon before sun-up and arrived just as Abe was coming from the barn in his bib overalls and rubber boots. They both headed to the house to eat breakfast.

The kitchen felt warm and comforting to Robert, after his hard, cold ride up the foggy mountain. Ethel Martin poured a cup of steaming hot coffee for each man and broke four eggs into the bacon grease bubbling in her iron skillet.

Robert had come to marry Louella Martin, who was upstairs in her bedroom trying to tame her frizzy blond hair enough to wear a veil. She was a skinny wisp of a girl with real big hair.

Ethel had made Louella's wedding dress from material she bought at Rose's Department store in Flat Rock. She had also sewn a light blue bridesmaid dress for her younger daughter, Dilly.

When Abe finished eating, he went to make a fire in the living room, where Ethel had placed two baskets of pink plastic flowers on either side of the fireplace.

Preacher Brown from Shady Grove Baptist church arrived right on time at eleven o'clock, little black Bible in hand, ready to get down to business. His forehead was covered with pimples from the oily Brylcreem he used to slick down his hair. He straightened his burgundy and green stripped tie, cleared his throat and in his deep, loud preacher voice said, "Let's begin."

Abe yelled up to his daughter, "Git yourself down here, Louella, Preacher Brown is ready to git you married."

All her life Louella had been resigned to the fact that when Abe Martin was your daddy and he told you to do something, you didn't ask questions. You did it as fast as you could. But Robert Stone was taking her away from all that "to live happily ever after." The only things she regretted leaving behind were her goats.

Robert was a supervisor at the Dixon Cotton Mill on Delburg Street. He was a very thrifty man, so by the age of thirty he had saved enough money to build a nice house on Main Street.

Louella had never ventured far from the mountain where she was born. When she arrived at her new house in Dixon, she felt like a trout that had jumped out of the Flat Rock River. That first day she was sitting on the sofa watching the late afternoon sun cast a cold blue shadow across her white wedding dress when Robert dropped her suitcase at her feet and said, "Louella, go fix my supper." And so it began.

Having just turned nineteen, she lived down the street from Dixon College, where young men came to learn and well-educated men came to teach, Louella Stone was a lost soul amongst them.

Robert, a well-respected man about town, made good money at the Dixon Cotton Mill and began buying property along Main Street. He rented his first site to a man who opened Dixon Deli, a popular place with the college students. A short time later, he bought the buildings that housed The College Cut Rate Pharmacy, The Town Gazette and The Jetton Barber Shop.

In Dixon there were two classes of people – the revered college group and the less admired "townies". Louella Stone didn't fit into either category. She was an outsider, never invited to join the local Bridge clubs, book clubs, nor even a church circle.

She had once felt useful milking cows and tending her beloved goats. Now, it seemed, her only reason for living was to do Robert's bidding. The only thing she ever asked for was a goat. He bought a pair and built a pen that extended all the way down to Jackson Street. He didn't do this to make his wife happy, but rather because goat's milk soothed his painful stomach.

Soon Robert purchased a building leased to Washam's Grocery Store, where Louella shopped for the food she cooked for her husband. Even there, she barely received a nod from George Washam.

The years passed slowly and nothing changed until two days after Robert turned fifty. That day she answered a knock on her door. It was a man from Dixon Cotton Mill, who had come with bad news. Robert was dead.

Suddenly, Louella Stone, the goat woman from flat rock, practically owned Dixon. Now she had nothing much to do except walk down Main Street past *her* stores, with *her* head held high. Now people nodded to *her* and said, "Good day, Miss Louella." But when she encountered the snooty college students, they would giggle to each other and whisper, "Look out, there goes that creepy-ass woman."

Louella wore the same dresses year after year. When she took her daily walks past her stores, she wore old lady comfort shoes and tan stockings darned with black thread. Her great head of hair, now gone white, was pulled back into a big frizzy bun on her neck.

She checked on each store every day. The townsfolk saw her walking home with all the unsold papers from the Gazette, which she added to the huge yellowed stacks on her front porch.

Louella Stone had money, lots of money, and everybody knew it. But she didn't spend it. Everybody also knew she buried it in fruit jars in the goats' pen.

Before Robert died, he had a bathroom built on the back porch right outside the kitchen. Louella seldom used it, but chose instead to go across the street and use the neighbor's. They were accustomed to her knocking on the door and announcing that she had come to use their bathroom.

Children walking home from school would stop in front of her house and yell, "Come out, Mrs. Witch. Where are you, Mrs. Witch?" Louella would stick her straggled mess of white hair out the door and yell like the hag of doom, "Git away from here, or I'm coming after you!"

On cold winter days, Louella would not spend money to heat her house. Instead, she went to the warm college library. She learned to love the smell of old books and enjoyed the peace and silence of the great hall. She was exposed to good literature for the first time. She found that reading was a way to escape her dismal life, if only in her head.

She spent hours, even days, in a soft chair next to the geography section. She dreamed of taking a train through Europe, a boat ride down the Danube, touring castles in England, climbing the Munro's in Scotland, seeing the snow covered mountains in Switzerland and hiking to the pyramids in Egypt.

One day Louella Stone just disappeared.

Some folks say they saw her board a train at the Dixon Depot. Nobody really knew where she went, they only knew she was gone. Vanished. For years people dug around her yard, hoping to find the buried fruit jars filled with money. If they had ever been there, well now, they were gone too.

MILDRED

You could set your watch by them, the truckers who started rolling into the parking lot of Bill's Grill at 6:30 AM.

Mildred's alarm buzzed at 5:00. She took the big pink plastic curlers out of her bleached blond hair, teased it a bit and sprayed it with extra strength hair spray before driving her faded blue Chevrolet down highway 115 to Bill's.

Bill was already there. He had the place nice and warm for their breakfast crowd.

It was the first of November and cold air had swept down from Canada during the night, bringing a slow drizzle mixed with sleet. It was still dark when the trucks started pulling into the muddy parking lot.

Mildred had made coffee so strong you could almost smell the color. She had a pot of grits on the back burner, bacon warming on the grill and biscuits browning in the oven.

One by one men wandered in, wiped their shoes on the door mat, shook sleet from their coats, sat on a stool at the counter and waited for a hot cup of coffee. But something was different today. There was a new face at the far end of the counter – a flirtatious smile swept across the stranger's face when Mildred brought him coffee.

"New in town?" she asked.

"Well, not really, darlin', new job though. Just got one with a new truckin' company. Makin' a run down to Atlanta today. Hell of a day to be goin' *anywhere,* if you ask me. My name's Richard, by the way."

"Well, I'm Mildred. Mighty nice to meet you, Richard."

Bill listened intently as he watched another pound of bacon sizzle on the grill. He and Mildred had grown up together and he was fiercely protective where she was concerned.

During breakfast the men told wild tales and laughed at each other's dirty jokes as Mildred made her rounds with her Pyrex coffee pot, refilling their cups. The men sopped their plates clean with their last biscuits, watched sleet bounce against the front window and lit cigarettes, trying to prolong the inevitable.

Finally, with a nice warm breakfast under his belt, Richard paid his bill and strolled over to the gumball machine beside the door. When a big purple ball came tumbling out, he shoved it in his jaw, winked at Mildred and mumbled, "Bye, darlin."

"You come again," Mildred yelled, "and be careful out there. Keep it between the ditches, sweetheart"

"You got it, darlin'. See you 'round."

About a week later, Richard showed up again for breakfast.

"Well, look what the cat dragged in!" Mildred laughed as she brought Richard a cup of coffee.

He winked. "Been missin' me, darlin'?"

Bill, annoyed at the flirtatious conversation, wiped his hands across his apron, removed a carton of eggs from the refrigerator, and with loud forceful cracks, broke six and slung them across the hot grill.

***

Several months later, the coffee she made early in the morning made Mildred sick. The bacon frying on the grill made her even sicker. She couldn't even keep a piece of toast down before she made a mad dash for the restroom.

Bill watched and waited for her to say something, but when she didn't, he finally asked, "Who's the daddy, Mildred?"

"What?"

"Who knocked you up Mildred?"

Finally, in a pathetic, sorrowful voice she confessed, "Richard."

Later that day, Bill was filling an order when Richard came in. "Take over," he told her as he went to confront Richard. Before the man had a chance to sit down, Bill grabbed him by the elbow and dragged him back outside.

By the time Richard staggered to his semi, his nose was bleeding profusely and he could barely see from his one eye that was still open.

***

Well, far as Mildred was concerned, they had to get married. Richard moved into his bride's rental house and brought along his mother, Gussie, who was crippled with arthritis and deaf as a pine stump.

Mildred continued to spend her days cooking at Bill's Grill, and when she came home late in the afternoons she started cooking for Richard and Gussie. Problem was, most afternoons by the time dinner was on the table, Richard was high on Wild Turkey and Gussie was high on pain pills.

The Wild Turkey finally got Richard in trouble. It caused him to drive his semi into the trestle down on South Main that held up the Southern Railroad overpass. Even worse, a train was crossing at the time. People were seriously injured—some real bad. The road and the overpass were closed for weeks until repairs could be made.

Richard went to prison, Gussie went to a nursing home and Mildred went into labor.

Richard Roosevelt Cook, Jr. came three weeks early, but he already weighed eight pounds and was more than ready to take on the world. Mildred's younger sister became his babysitter so Mildred could go back to work

Little Ricky Cook was as mischievous as they come. He stole his share of watermelons from the neighbors, candy from Doc Anderson's store, and got into fistfights with his cousins, who were his teachers in crime.

Ricky changed, though, when he started to school and began reading. Then you would likely find him in some quiet corner with his nose in a book. Bill, who had become his father figure, taught him how to hunt, fish and be a man in the world. He taught Ricky to drive and bought him an old truck. He gave him a job at the grill earning money, while his cousins were getting caught for speeding and arrested for DUI's.

Mildred knew her son was smart and wanted to go to college. All through the years she had pinched pennies working at the grill and she had put money aside, so when he was accepted at the University of North Carolina, she paid his tuition.

Mildred and Bill continued cooking the best breakfasts in the area and the best lunches anywhere. People drove miles to get one of Bill's burgers.

But as Bill neared retirement, he began having health problems. Years of breathing cigarette smoke – his and his customers—was more than his lungs could handle. Mildred talked him into selling the grill and she took him home with her. It was her turn to look after him.

Ricky graduated from college and took a job teaching creative writing. He wanted to be a writer, and every night after teaching, he wrote.

After two years of hard work, his book found a publisher and went to the printers. He called his mother and told her it would soon be in bookstores. He hadn't said much about it, and she hadn't asked. She was never much of a reader and figured she wouldn't understand his work anyway. So she didn't think much about it until one afternoon, when she and Bill had just finished lunch, someone knocked on her door.

The woman said, "I'm from the Mecklenburg News and I'm here about your son's book. I'm writing a review for Sunday's News. Are you Mildred Cook?"

"Yes, I am, but my son's not here."

"Oh, I know," the woman replied. "But Ricky's publisher sent me an early edition of his book to review, and it's *you* I want to interview, Mrs. Cook."

The woman handed Mildred the book.

Her heart skipped a beat when she saw the cover – there, framed in gold, was her picture – and written beneath it in big bold black letters, was THE BEST MAMA IN THE WORLD and Other Stories by Ricky Cook.

PLATO

She was a teeny tiny woman who lived in a teeny tiny house and raised teeny tiny chickens that laid teeny tiny eggs. That was Plato Kerr. She raised Bantams mostly, and some Rock Island Reds.

Her house didn't have a front porch and not much of a back porch. The first thing you noticed was the tall lightning rods with white balls that stood at attention on either end of the roof. The house was plain, white, tall and skinny, much like Plato herself—no waist, no hips, no bosom. She had trouble keeping her underpants up. They just kept sliding down her skinny little bottom and she kept reaching around and yanking them up.

One leg was shorter than the other. She walked with a limp, which made her problem worse.

Plato was approaching her 40th birthday and had never been married. She took care of her parents until they died. The Kerr's lived up the road, right outside Dixon.

Millie, who lived in town, was in Doc Anderson's grocery store one day staring at the candy inside the glass enclosed counter, trying to make up her mind what to buy with her nickel, when Doc tapped his restless hands on the counter and said, "Make up your mind, girl, this ain't no museum, and I ain't got all day."

Then Plato, who had ridden her bike to town to sell her eggs, limped into the store with her basket on her arm. "Good mornin', Doc. I brung you some fresh eggs. There's two dozen in all."

Doc, a fat man with a shiny bald head, looked from beneath his enormous black eyebrows, rolled a stubby cigar from one side of his thin mouth to the other, wiped his hands on his dirty white apron, took the basket and started counting each egg to be sure he wasn't getting cheated. Then he opened the cash register and handed Plato some money.

She dropped it in her pocket, reached around her waist, hiked up her panties and limped to the front of the store. She was getting ready to go out when she turned and asked Doc if he knew anyone who took in sewing.

"Yeah, I do," he said. "Janie Cashion. Talk to Millie here, she knows Janie."

Plato limped around the baskets of dried beans to where Millie was unwrapping the Sugar Daddy sucker she had just bought. "Do you know where Janie lives?" she asked.

"Yeah, I live close to her," Millie said, "Want me to take you over there?"

"Yeah," Plato answered, yanked at her panties and limped outside to her bike.

Janie was sitting on the back-porch stringing beans when they arrived. She offered them a chair and a glass of sweet tea. Millie took a lapful of beans and started stringing and breaking them into a bowl nearby.

"I've come to see can you make me a dress," Plato said. "I can't find nothin' to fit me."

"Well, I can see that plain enough," Janie replied matter-of-factly. She went in the house and came back with a measuring tape, wrapped it around Plato's tiny little waist and then her chest, which was just another flat place except a little higher up.

"I have a closet full of leftover material," Janie said. "Come back in a week and I'll have you a dress made."

When Plato got home that day she knew immediately something wasn't right. Somebody had been in her house. She just knew it! It didn't smell right. She hiked up her panties and limped to the kitchen. The Kerrs had never locked their doors. If there ever was a key, Plato had never seen it.

She took her egg basket to the kitchen and looked at the apple pie she had baked that morning and left on the table to cool. Half of it was gone. Beside it was a handful of pecans.

Plato walked outside to check on her chickens. They were in the pen clucking and pecking for a nice little worm that might be hiding somewhere beneath the dirt, but one chicken was missing.

That night, as soon as she dropped off to sleep and began dreaming, a voice in her dream said, *Who stole your chicken, Plato?*

"I don't know!" she screamed in terror. "But he better watch out, 'cause I may kill him. Nobody messes with my chickens and gets away with it." She found her daddy's pistol in a bureau drawer and put it under her pillow.

A week later, she got up early, baked a nice loaf of bread and left for Janie's. Her dress was ready. It was light blue with daisies on it. Their little gold centers brought out the gold in her blond hair.

When she got home, someone had eaten half her loaf of bread and left a handful of wild strawberries on the table. *That's it,* she thought, *I have to get new locks put on my doors.*

Plato went outside to the chicken house and counted the chickens. Another one was missing.

That night she had trouble falling asleep, but as soon she dropped off the voice in her dream came again. *Plato, who stole your chickens?*

Early one morning Plato gathered her eggs and set out for Doc Anderson's store. This time she didn't leave anything out for the intruder to eat, but when she got home she found a bunch of grapes on the table, her new bottle of milk was half empty, some of the hoop cheese in the tin near the sink was gone as well as the leftover bread in the breadbox.

Then she heard someone moaning outside the back door and there she found a man, lying in a pool of blood.

Now it was against Plato's Methodist religion to curse, but this time she couldn't help herself. "Jesus M. McChrist," she yelled, I finally caught you, you thief!"

He had a deep gash in his left leg and was bleeding profusely. "I'm going to call the police," she said.

"Oh no, please ma'am. I can explain what happened."

"Well, Mr. Chicken Thief, you got a lot of explainin' to do."

He was bleeding so badly, she knew something had to be done. She made a tourniquet with her belt and placed it above the wound. Then she cleaned it with soapy water and bandaged it.

"'It hurts. I can't walk," he moaned.

"Well, I'm gonna' call a doctor."

"No, please ma'am. I'll be fine."

"What happened to you?"

"I was rushing and tripped over that axe you keep propped near the back door."

"Well, serves you right, you chicken thief. You ought to be in jail, and you're gonna be as soon as I call the police."

"Oh, my God help me. Please don't call the police. I can explain everything!"

She knew a Christian woman like herself should say something nice to him, but she truly didn't give a damn. "Shut up and tell me what you did with my chickens."

Plato helped him inside as he mumbled, "I'm sorry. I can explain everything." Then he closed his eyes and drifted off.

Plato covered him with a quilt and sat down to think what to do next. For some reason she didn't quite understand, she just sat there and stared at him.

When he finally opened his eyes, she saw they were the color of the Carolina blue skies. Just about the prettiest eyes she had ever seen.

"What's your name?" she asked angrily.

"It's Tate. I'm so tired. I can explain everything."

"Well, I don't want to hear it. You've lost a lot of blood. I'm callin' the doctor."

"No, please. I'll leave."

"Well, you can't walk, so just shut up." Plato got some leftover penicillin tablets from the medicine cabinet and some aspirin for the pain, gave him one of each, then covered him with a warm quilt.

He woke up the next morning to the smell of hot coffee perking and biscuits in the oven. It had been a very long time since he had eaten.

After a nice breakfast of biscuits and tiny little Bantam eggs, he told her he had been living at her tenant house down in her woods.

"Well, Jesus M. McChrist, why?" she shouted.

"Well, I can explain it all. But now with this hurt leg, I…..."

"I don't give a flyin' flip about your leg," she yelled. Yet he couldn't walk, he was still bleeding and obviously in pain. She saw tears in his pretty blue eyes. What else could she do but let him sleep on the pallet until she had time to think it through?

Again, Plato cleaned his wound with peroxide, wrapped it with clean gauze bandages and gave him more penicillin and aspirin.

That night the dream voice said, *Who's that chicken thief in your house, Plato?*

She jumped straight up and shouted, "Jesus M. McChrist. Will you just shut up? His name is Tate, and I'm trying to think how in the devil I'm gonna get rid of him."

Plato kept the wound clean and changed his bandages. He would look at her with those blue eyes, bat his long black lashes, smile and say, "You're a mighty fine woman. God bless you."

Plato urged him to stand on his leg, but he cried out in pain. She poured him a glass of her daddy's fine whisky and gave him an aspirin before she brought him a nice warm bowl of chicken soup.

***

"I want you to make me a wedding dress," Plato said when she went to see Janie a few weeks later.

"Oh, my goodness! You gettin' married, honey? Who you marrying?" Janie asked.

"Well, you don't know him. He ain't from around here. He's kind of bashful. Don't want nobody to know his business."

"Y'all having a church wedding?" Janie asked.

"No, I'm gonna get Preacher Collier from over at the Methodist church to marry us at home. Soon as you get done with my dress."

"Give me a week," Janie said.

When the bride-to-be went to Doc Anderson's, she was all smiles when she handed him a basket of eggs. "Gettin' married," she announced.

Doc was counting out her money when the door opened. The sheriff came in with a frowning, mean-looking woman with three little girls.

"I'm lookin' for a man called Tate McNeely," the sheriff said in a loud, commanding voice. "He's wanted for child abandonment."

"Well, Jesus M. McChrist!" Plato cursed before hiking up her underpants and limping out the front door as fast as she could go.

"I'm turning your sorry ass in!" she yelled at Tate when she got home. "The sheriff is goin' around town lookin' for you, you cheater. Your wife came in Doc Anderson's with your poor little girls. You're wanted for child abandonment."

Tears filled his pretty blue eyes. "Plato, I swear on a stack of Bibles that woman ain't my wife, and them girls ain't my kids. You have to believe me."

"Now how in this world am I supposed to believe you? You been livin' in my tenant house, breakin' in my house, stealin' my chickens, drinkin' my daddy's liquor, eatin' my cookin' and lettin' me wait on you."

"Please Plato, I can explain everything," he begged.

***

When Plato Kerr went back to Janie's and tried on the wedding dress, it was so beautiful—a perfect fit. She was ecstatic. Just what she had dreamed about all her life—being a bride and getting married in a dress like that.

She called preacher Collier and planned the date on her birthday: August 29th, her forty-first birthday. Janie and Millie offered to help with a reception.

Plato baked herself a wedding cake, made punch with ginger ale and orange juice and mints tinted pale green. Janie brought salted peanuts she bought at Doc Anderson's. The dining room table was covered with the tablecloth Plato's mother had crocheted and left in her hope chest.

Millie cut the last of the summer roses and made a bouquet for Plato to carry when she said "I do" to Tate McNeely.

Plato sent Tate to wait in the tenant house, explaining it was bad luck to see the bride before the wedding.

Janie pulled Plato's hair on top of her head and added a little veil. She rubbed a soft beige base over her face and then a dusting of soft beige powder. She added some rose rouge and lipstick. Finally, Janie brushed mascara over Plato's pale eyelashes.

Millie handed Plato the bouquet of white roses just as Pastor Collier and his wife, Janelle, came in. Everyone assembled in the parlor awaiting Tate's arrival.

They waited, and waited, and waited.

Pastor Collier went out back to call Tate, then he walked down to the tenant house to find him. It was nearly 3:00 when he returned. "Tate's gone, Miss Kerr," he said incredulously. "He's not here anywhere."

Plato started sobbing. Her mascara made little black streaks beneath her eyes. The new hair-do came undone and fell loose around her shoulders and the newly applied makeup ran in little rivulets down her cheeks. She hiked up her panties and limped to the sofa, where she plopped down with an undignified thud.

"Well, Jesus M. McChrist," she cried as she wiped her nose on the sleeve of her beautiful white satin wedding dress.

Just then the sheriff and Tate came in. The sheriff said, "Sorry, Miss Kerr. Hope I didn't get the groom here too late. I expect you were wondering where he went."

"Yes!" Plato yelled angrily."

"I'm so sorry, Plato," Tate said. "My son is married to the she-devil from hell, the woman you saw at Doc Anderson's. Tate, Jr. just took all he could stand of that woman and he ran away several weeks ago. I found him living in your little tenant house. He's the one been stealin' your food and your chickens. I chased him up to your house and tried to stop him from stealin'. That's how I tripped over your axe. Junior just ran away and left me there bleeding.

"I've been tryin' to talk him into goin' home. I finally turned him in myself and he's back home now. The sheriff had a long talk with my daughter-in-law, and she knows she has to mend her ways."

"Now, Miss Kerr," the sheriff said, "I can sympathize with having to put up with a woman like Junior's wife. Tate here has been through hell, but he's done the right thing. He's a good man. Now you can file breakin' and enterin' charges if you're of a mind to, or you can just get on with your weddin'."

Plato Kerr was in shock. She was hardly aware of Millie wiping make-up off her face or Janie putting loose strands of hair back in place. But she did feel Tate's warm hand in hers, helping her off the sofa and taking her to stand with him in front of Pastor Collier. She heard the pastor say, "Do you take this man to be your lawfully wedded husband?"

She was about to say *Jesus M. McChrist YES,* but caught herself. She squeezed Tate's hand and whispered, "I do

ROXIE

Apartment 320, located on the third floor of the retirement home had been cleaned, laundry done and the spoiled rotten old white woman, Mrs. Stinson, was sitting in front of the TV watching the local news. She had a tray on her lap with the lunch I had brought up from the café downstairs.

Nothing about it suited her. She swore up and down that I didn't get what she ordered. She yelled for me to bring the salt shaker from her kitchen. Then she wanted me to heat her chicken in the microwave, make her a cup of coffee, get more sugar from the top shelf in the left hand cabinet, and then just as I was about to sit down for a minute, she yelled, "Get me some more cream for my coffee."

Oh, my God how I wanted to scream. But I managed instead to walk out on her balcony, where I pounded my fist on the railing.

Looking out across the lawn, I watched a man on a riding mower going back and forth grooming the well-manicured grass. The landscaping helped make the home just the kind of prestigious place where people with enough money would come to spend their last days.

The grounds had to look just as lovely as the photos in the expensive brochures promised. The home's PR firm printed and mailed these brochures to prospective residents like Mrs. Stinson in there bitching about her chicken.

They advertised a golf course that was the picture of perfection. I could see it off in the distance. A foursome marched their little cleated feet up to the eighth hole and prepared to tee off.

For those who preferred tennis, the courts were to one side of the golf course, and on the other was a lake well stocked with brim and bass.

When I was a girl, all this land belonged to Miss Roxie. I picked cotton where those men hit their little white balls.

All kinds of memories came flooding back. These people here now didn't know nothin' about good eatin' because they never ate Miss Roxie's cookin'.

Miss Roxie owned every acre this place was built on. She couldn't afford to live here now, and I guess they wouldn't even let a black woman in the front door if she walked up today. She didn't have a lot of money in the bank, but her children sure pulled in a load when they sold her land.

Like I said, Miss Roxie didn't have much money, but Lord, she was one happy women. And she shared her joy with every livin' soul who entered her door.

I could see it from here - the very spot where her house used to sit. It had a big front porch with a swing painted green and a railing wide enough to hold all her potted ferns, geraniums, petunias and marigolds.

There were three rooms, but the one she called her "sittin room" served as a living room and sewing room, with her bed in one corner. She made all her clothes and aprons from pretty printed flour sacks. Each apron had a bonnet to match.

Behind her home was her cook house, with a breezeway and porch between the two buildings. Cookin' and feedin' people brought her more happiness than anything money could ever buy.

She ran her kitchen like a fine restaurant, preparing food on an old wood stove in quantities large enough to feed an army.

She had three sons, Freeman, Gordan and Tootie. The two oldest boys ran the farm, planted cotton, vegetables and cared for the livestock. They were married with children of their own.

Tootie, her baby boy, was kinda' strange. He just never grew up the way he was supposed to. But Lord knows, he could snap green beans, shell peas and shuck corn like nobody's business. Miss Roxie fixed him a chair and a table on the back porch which she declared was his very own space. Tootie had this expression he used all the time: "Well, I'll say."

Freeman was bad to drink, and he and Gordon fought a lot. I remember them fussing. Gordon would say, "Freeman, you turned out to be about the sorriest asshole I ever seen. You are the fuckup of all fuckups, and if you don't stop drinkin' that rot gut, you gonna to be the deadest fuckup I ever seen."

My sisters and I picked cotton for Miss Roxie. I remember one time when the sky was slowly lightin' to the beginnings of the day and the first red rays of the sun were just comin' up over the cotton patch. We started pickin' and picked all morning until it was time to stop for dinner.

While we waited to eat, I pulled a bucket of water out of the well and gave each of my sisters a dipperful. We sat on the back steps just breathing in all the good smells comin' out of that kitchen.

Gordon and two of his children were there, along with one of Freeman's kids. Gordon sat under the walnut tree. I watched him hand roll a cigarette and light up while we waited for Miss Roxie to yell, "Y'all come eat."

I could hear Miss Roxie humming *Amazing Grace*, while the pots and pans rattled on her cook stove. When the oven door opened, it let out smells that were almost more than a hungry stomach could tolerate.

All of a sudden Miss Roxie hollered, "Tootie, come git your goat outta this here kitchen. How am I 'spose to cook with that damn thing a gittin' in my way?"

Tootie stood up and said, "Well, I say." He scratched himself, then went to get the goat, along with two chickens that had strolled in to peck at any little tidbits dropped on the floor.

When we were called in to eat, Miss Roxie pulled a pan of sweet potatoes from the oven. Steamy, sweet juice burst from slits in the orange skins of the potatoes laid in rows across her pan. Two cast iron pans of cornbread rested on the back of the stove. A pot of green beans and corn seasoned with a slab of fatback was placed to one side. Two fried chickens and gravy to pour over the biscuits were waiting in the warming closet. A dish of freshly churned butter was on the table, along with a plate of sliced tomatoes and cantaloupe wedges. If we had any room left, a washtub full of banana pudding awaited us.

That day stands out in my mind because it was the day Gordon said, "Mama, I been looking at a TV downtown at Mr. Weaver's electrical shop. When I get paid for this last load of cotton, I'll have enough money to get it for you."

Tootie had just slathered a piece of cornbread with butter when he heard this, and he dropped it on the floor. A chicken standing in the doorway had been waiting for this opportunity, and she tore out across the floor racing Tootie for the tidbit.

"When you gittin' it Gordon?" Tootie asked.

"It's a surprise," Gordon said.

Two days later, we were sittin' down to Miss Roxie's dinner of country ham, red eye gravy on fluffy white rice, corn on the cob, field peas, biscuits, deviled eggs, sweet tea and blackberry dumplings when Gordon told us he had the TV in his truck.

"Let's set it up!" yelled Tootie.

Gordon brought it in and put it on top of his Mama's console radio. It was just a little ole box – RCA, as I recall. Tootie reached up and switched it on. It made an awful screeching noise while a bunch of little white dots danced all over the screen. "Well, I say, this dad burn thing ain't no count," Tootie grumbled.

"It needs an antenna up on the roof, and I got one in the truck," Gordon replied. "You girls go on out to the cotton patch. I'll have it up when you get done this afternoon."

The hours passed like slow molasses poured from a fruit jar, but finally five o'clock came. I emptied my cotton sack into the wagon and we raced to the house. "It's up," I shouted. "The antenna's on the chimney."

Miss Roxie had spread blankets all around the floor in front of the TV. She brought us a pitcher of Kool-Aid and a plate of nilla wafers.

"I done watched Howdy Doody," Tootie bragged.

We could only get two channels, but we watched Joey the Clown and Fred Kirby. Tootie got up and pulled at his pants that had gotten all wadded up in his bottom. He stuck out his purple grape Kool-Ade tongue and said, "Well, I say, there's Hop-Along Cassidy. I thought he lived downtown. I see him down there all the time."

"That ain't Hop-Along Cassidy," I said. "That's just that mean old policeman who makes faces at us."

We spent many hours in front of that little magical RCA TV watching Sky King, Annie Oakley and The Jackson Five on the Ed Sullivan show. That was the first time we ever saw kids like us on TV.

I took my cotton pickin' money and the money I made from selling black berries down to Johnny Brown's Department Store. I bought a pair of shoes, a new pair of sunglasses and some bubble gum and jaw breakers for Tootie.

I was still lost in a world of memories, when I heard old Mrs. Stinson yellin', "Get yourself in here. I don't pay you to sit out there and daydream. What were you thinking about anyway?"

"Happy times, Mrs. Stinson. Happy times."

TONI

The pain was excruciating. She had screamed until her lungs hurt. Now someone was wheeling her into the delivery room and telling her a nurse was coming to give her something for pain.

Julia Trent had been in the hospital labor room since Anthony brought her around midnight. It seemed like it had been days—not hours—and now, finally, she was on a cart moving down a hallway. A slight breeze brushed over her as she was whisked through a door and transferred to a table beneath a blinding white light.

A nurse stood in front of a large window, where the morning sun was rising on a new day – her son's birthday.

The needle went into her lower back, delivering almost instant relief. The room began revolving and the voices between her legs chatted like it was just another day at the office.

"Here it comes!" Someone said. "Okay, it's cleaned up. Weighs eight pounds."

Julia heard the cries and raised her head to see a nurse wrapping the baby in a blanket.

"You have a beautiful, healthy little girl, Mrs. Trent."

"No!" Julia cried. "I need a boy – a boy for Anthony."

Anthony had gone to meet a friend. He was too busy discussing a business deal to give any thought to what might be happening to his wife. When he finally returned to the hospital, it was early afternoon. He lied about having been tied up at the office, then lied again about needing to hurry back to meet a deadline.

Later that afternoon, a woman came to Julia's room to fill out the birth certificate. "What is the baby's name?" she asked.

"Anthony," Julia replied.

"But it's a girl," the woman responded.

"I know what it is," Julia replied angrily. "The baby's name is Anthony."

Anthony Trent didn't give a darn about his baby. It was Julia's idea anyway, and she could bloody well take care of it. He had better things to do.

On her first day at school, the defiant six-year-old informed her teacher that her name was Toni, not Anthony. She said her mother didn't tell her what to wear or how to do her hair. She said she would read only the library books she liked, or write her own.

By the time Toni reached her teen years, she refused to live by her father's misogynistic, bigoted rules, believing they were wrong. His belt slashes across her back didn't change a thing.

When she entered high school, Toni Trent was a self-confident young woman with a plan for a better life. She was going to college.

That idea was quickly discouraged by her parents, who believed the only thing every woman needed was a man, a good Christian man.

Luckily, a supportive teacher suggested Toni could work her way through college and helped her make those arrangements.

Dressed in a starched white waitress uniform, Toni was in the college dining hall every afternoon at 5pm, carrying heavy trays to her assigned table.

Toni seldom went home for visits, because she felt unwelcome. When she did, Anthony snarled like a wild animal, "Who the hell do you think you are?" he growled. "You ain't nothin' but a damn hippy dippy."

Julia Trent sat by like the battered housewife she was and agreed with every word he said.

Occasionally Toni wrote her parents, but got no response: no *how are you, do you need money, when are you coming home or we miss you*. Nothing. So after a while, she didn't give a damn.

When Toni went home again, she invited her parents to attend her graduation. Anthony Trent stared at his daughter with steely blue eyes that were frightening. Was he high, she wondered? He sounded stoned. Besides being a Class- A dick, was he also doing drugs?

After Toni got a degree in journalism, she was awarded a scholarship to study communications and an apprenticeship as a researcher on a TV series.

Then came the call from Julia to inform her that her "poor father" had landed in prison for selling drugs. Suddenly Julia Trent became very interested in her daughter.

Toni had started writing a book, more or less as an experiment, but it took on a life of its own. On a dare, she sent it to a publisher. Soon *Unforgotten,* a historical romance novel, was a best seller in book stores.

Now that she had money, Toni began sending her mother a check every month, but never got a thank you in return.

Two years later, the second book in the *Unforgotten* series was published.

Anthony Trent died in prison. Toni went home to bury his ashes, clean out the house and find a suitable retirement home for her mother.

Then something unexpected happened. Matt Moore, the executive producer of Cameo Studios, called to buy the rights to *Unforgotten* for a TV series.

"Have your attorney contact us, if you are interested," he said.

Toni landed at LaGuardia two hours before her meeting and took a taxi to Cameo Studios.

"You understand the films will not be exactly like your books, because your content will need to be condensed," Matt said. "We reserve the right to make changes, but we will try to keep the spirit you intended. You will be a consultant, and we welcome your suggestions.

"Our casting director studied many audition tapes," he continued, "and we have hired the actors to play Abby and Alex."

In a dark room on a large screen, Toni watched clouds drift across an orange sun setting behind blue green water. A soft, throaty voice began singing *Memories light the corners of my mind. Misty water colored memories of the way we were. Scattered pictures of the smiles we left behind. Smiles we gave each other for the way we were.*

Based on books by Toni Trent rolled across the bottom of the screen in big white script, followed by *Matt Moore, executive producer, Alicia Scott as Abby and Jason Monroe as Alex.*

After the episode ended and the lights came on, Matt turned to Toni, "What do you think, Miss Trent?"

"My God!" she gasped.

"We have the best screen writers, costume designers and set designers in the business," he told her. "Cameo Studios hires only the finest sound techs and cinematographers. You can rest assured our productions are first class."

"Yes, I can see that," she said.

"I want you to meet our writers. Come along with me to the writer's room, and then we'll visit the set so you can meet the actors. After that Miss Trent, will you allow me to take you to dinner?"

Matt Moore always dressed very casually and wore his curly hair rather long. Toni was aware of its woodsy smell as he helped her into the cab.

They toasted *Unforgotten* and Cameo Studios. She found him easy to be with. They laughed together like old friends as they ate and watched the snow falling outside.

"Tomorrow I'll introduce you to Mr. Drew, Cameo's president, and after that, I have a surprise for you."

The Cameo caterer had set up a luncheon for Matt and Toni along with Alicia and Jason, who played Abby and Alex.

Making a rather dramatic entrance, Alicia blew a kiss, Jason kissed Toni and called her "Sweets."

They drank Riesling in crystal glasses with the Cameo emblem etched on the side. They were served a tossed salad, warm crab cakes with caper sauce, miniature muffins and a fruit tart with ice cream.

During lunch, Jason kept his hand on Alicia's knee and called her "Hon". She gave him a light kiss on the cheek and teased him about his recent "blooper" during filming. It occurred during a scene when he was costumed in a traditional Scottish kilt.

"Jason went to the rest room and dropped his modesty patch in the urinal!" Alicia laughed. "The filming crew howled when he came out holding paper towels over his you-know-what."

"And if that didn't give them reason enough to laugh…" Alicia continued mercilessly, "when we started the love scene again and I kissed Jason, he farted!"

Toni, somewhat embarrassed by the personal banter, couldn't wait to ask Matt if the two actors were an item.

"Oh, yeah, off and on. You know how actors are," Matt told her. "Whichever way the wind is blowing, they play musical beds."

"Oh well, that's normal, I suppose." Toni blushed. "But they are perfect as Abby and Alex."

The first season of *Unforgotten* aired and created unbelievable numbers of fans. When work began on season two, Toni moved to New York to be closer to the studios and to Matt. Actually, she moved in with Matt.

"That's a wrap!" someone shouted. Cheers went up from the whole crew working on the eighteenth century set, inspiring a wild celebration.

To top it off, a priest wearing a white wig and dressed in a period robe stepped in front of the fake castle. Abby and Alex, still in costume, moved beside him. A young boy quietly lit candles, and a little girl scattered rose petals down a walkway. Bright lights strobed from the catwalks overhead and mikes on long poles descended. The sound crew began playing the wedding march as Matt and Toni entered the set, also in costume, amid deafening applause. Their wedding rivaled anything ever filmed for TV, Hollywood or the soap operas.

Toni realized she was living inside one of her own romance novels.

***

Julia had yelled so long her lungs hurt. The pain was excruciating.

"I'm right here," the nurse said. "I brought a shot for your pain. It'll be better in a few minutes, and then I'll take you to the TV room."

Unforgotten had been nominated for a Golden Globe for the best TV drama series. Extra chairs had been added to the Rest Awhile Retirement Home TV room, so that the residents as well as the staff could watch.

Julia was wheeled in and given a special place in the front row. Other residents and the staff took seats, while others had to stand against the wall.

Once everyone was seated and the room got quiet, the long-awaited program came on the large TV screen. An orchestra opened with a powerful fanfare, neon lights flashed over an elaborate set. Cameras panned the glamourous audience dressed in gorgeous outfits and jewelry. Then the MC, a short, balding comedian, told several funny jokes bringing the audience to their feet with applause.

The best actress award was presented, the best supporting actor and several others before the executive producer of last year's winner of best TV drama series appeared and made a few funny comments before announcing this year's nominees.

He fumbled around trying to open the envelope, stood still a moment in breathtaking silence, smiled and then said, "*Unforgotten.*"

The orchestra began playing *Memories light the corners of my mind. Misty water colored memories of the way we were.* The audience burst into a round of applause. Matt, dragging Toni by the hand, bounded onto the stage followed by Alicia and Jason and the whole production crew. Toni was beautiful in a low cut black designer dress and the diamond necklace Matt had given her for a wedding present.

Matt stood close to the mike and said, "This is all due to the talented, inspiring writer of the *Unforgotten* books and my lovely wife, Toni Trent."

The Rest Awhile Retirement Home reverberated with cheers. Suddenly, Julia Trent was a celebrity, surrounded by people waiting to shake her hand.

This was the happiest day of her life. She forgot about the cancer in her left lung. "That's my girl!" She beamed into the cameras flashing all around her and tried to remember why on God's green earth she had ever wanted a son.

About the Author

Betsey Barber Hampton lives in Davidson, North Carolina, the prototype for the fictional Dixon. Much of her adult life she was a professional artist and loved showing her works at various galleries.

Now in her eighties and handicapped, Betsey enjoys writing short stories reflective of her experiences growing up in the rural south in the mid to late Twentieth Century.

These stories are about strong women who were not recognized or appreciated for their strengths. Some were strong because they had to be. Others were born with minds and skills that refused to be oppressed, and none of them should be forgotten.

OTHER SHORT STORY COLLECTIONS

FULL CIRCLE

A TIME and a PLACE

FAMILY SECRETS

www.ingramcontent.com/pod-product-compliance
Lightning Source LLC
Chambersburg PA
CBHW071409170626
46811CB00003B/1324